BEST SERVED DEAD

Patti Petrone Miller

The scanning, uploading, and distribution of this book via the Internet or via any other means without the permission of the publisher or the author is illegal and punishable by law. Please purchase only authorized electronic editions, and do not participate in or encourage electronic piracy of copyrighted materials. Your support of the author's rights is appreciated.

This is a work of fiction. Names, characters, places, brands, media, and incidents either are the product of the author's imagination or are used fictitiously. Any resemblance to actual events or locales or persons, living or dead, is entirely coincidental.

BEST SERVED DEAD

Copyright © 2024 by Patti Petrone Miller

All rights reserved. This book or any portion thereof may not be reproduced or used in any manner whatsoever without the express written permission of the publisher except for the use of brief quotations in a book review.

First Edition
First Printing, 2024
AP Miller Productions

Book List

Welcome to Scarecrow Hollow
The Pendleton Witches
The Boogeyman
The Cabinet of Curiosities
Love In Stitches
Accidental Vows
Sin Takes A Holiday

Where to find Patti Online

Pinterest: https://www.pinterest.com/pattipetmiller
Tiktok: tiktok.com/@pattipetronemillerauthor
Facebook: https://www.facebook.com/pattipetronemiller/
Facebook: https://facebook.com/elliotandjosephthumbsup?
Facebook: https://www.facebook.com/groups/1242845583217091/
Website: www.patti-petrone-miller-executive-producer.ueniweb.com
Website: http://pattipage0325.wixsite.com/patti-petrone-miller
Threads: pattipetronemiller@threads.com

Recipes

Googly Eyeball Soup

Ingredients

    3 shallots
    400 g chopped tomato (natural or canned)
    260 g of vegetable broth
    30 g of cream for cooking
    20 g olive oil
    Sugar
    Salt and pepper
    10 pieces of fresh cheese or "Burguitos"
    black olives
    Preparation
    1.   Peel and chop the shallots.
    2.   Add the oil and fry for 6 minutes
    3.   Add the tomato and the broth
    4.   Blend until smooth using a mixer
    5.   Add the cream and a pinch of sugar, heat for 3 minutes and season with salt and pepper.
    6.   While preparing the googly eyes. Drain the olives and cut them into slices. Place the central slices, the ones with the largest hole, on top of each piece of fresh cheese.
    6. Pour the soup into individual bowls and distribute about 5 pieces of cheese with olives in each portion.
    7. Serve right away.

Brain Pasta

Ingredients
- 14oz. (400g) of pumpkin or squash
- A little bit of butter for the pan
- 1 onion
- 3 garlic cloves
- 7 oz. (200g) of bacon
- Salt, pepper, grounded cilantro seeds ...
- 1 tbs of curry pasta
- 1/2 tsp of hot paprika (optional)
- Grounded nutmeg
- Oregano
- 0,4 US cup (100ml) of white wine
- 14 oz. (400gr) of black spaghetti
  - 0,4 US cup (100ml) of liquid cream
  - Parsley
  - Parmesan cheese at your taste

Witches Brew Stew

Instructions

1. Start by preparing the pumpkin: the best way is to cut slices of 1 inches, and remove the skin of each piece with a knife. Then cut the slices in small cubes.
2. Heat a little bit of butter in a big pan over medium heat, chop the onion and 2 garlic cloves in the meantime and throw them into the pan once the butter is hot. Cook them until soft, 5 minutes more or less.
3. Add the bacon in the pan and cook until it is fried.
4. Incorporate the pumpkin's cubes, the salt, pepper, grounded cilantro, the curry paste, the hot paprika and the nutmeg and

mix well. Cook for a couple of minutes, until you smell the spices.

5.   Pour the white wine in the pan, cover and simmer until the pumpkin is soft and can be mashed with a fork, about 20 minutes.

In the meantime, start cooking the pasta as indicated on the pack.

    1.Drain the water of the pasta when they are ready and place them into a large platter.

    2.Once the pumpkin sauce is ready, roughly mash the pieces with a fork, but don't forget to leave a few pieces so that the pasta will look like Halloween brain pasta!

    3.Incorporate the cream and the parmesan cheese.

    4.Pour the pumpkin cream on the pasta, and top it with a little bit of chopped parsley, trying to keep all the colors separated for the presentation.

    5.Then mix it in front of the guest so that the black and orange are mixing together into a brain pasta!!!

BEST SERVED DEAD
by Patti Petrone Miller

AP Miller Productions

Patti Petrone Miller

CHAPTER 1

Morty's brown tousled hair crackled with static as he tied on his bat-winged apron. He grinned at his reflection in the kitchen's polished steel surface. Perfect. The annual Hollow Creek Halloween Festival was his time to shine.

"Let's get cookin', ghouls and boils!" he called out to his staff. "We've got hungry monsters to feed!"

His sous chef, Belinda, rolled her eyes but smiled. "What's on the menu today, boss?"

Morty's eyes gleamed. "Oh, you're in for a treat. Or should I say, a trick?"

He pulled out a tray of what looked like severed fingers. The nails were perfectly manicured.

"Witch's Finger Cookies!" he announced proudly. "Complete with almond slivers for nails and raspberry jam for that freshly severed look."

Belinda leaned in, impressed. "They look disturbingly real."

"That's the idea, my dear," Morty chuckled. "Now, let's get these out to our unsuspecting victims—er, customers."

As they exited the kitchen, the bustling atmosphere of The Ghoulish Gourmet enveloped them. Patrons chatted excitedly, their voices mingling with the clink of silverware and the occasional theatrical scream.

Morty approached a table where a young couple sat, looking both excited and apprehensive.

"Welcome to The Ghoulish Gourmet!" he grinned. "I hope you're prepared for a dining experience to die for."

The woman giggled nervously. "We've heard so much about this place."

"All good things, I hope," Morty winked. "Now, may I interest you in our special of the day? It's to die for—literally!"

He presented the platter of Witch's Finger Cookies with a flourish. The couple gasped, equal parts horrified and intrigued.

Morty's heart swelled with pride. This was why he loved his job. The perfect balance of fear and delight, served up on a silver platter.

As he returned to the kitchen, his mind raced with new ideas. The festival was his chance to truly showcase his talents. He'd need something spectacular, something that would leave everyone screaming—with joy, of course.

Little did he know, the upcoming festival would involve screams of an entirely different nature.

The autumn breeze carried the scent of pumpkin spice and decay through Hollow Creek's winding streets. Orange and black streamers fluttered from lampposts, their shadows dancing on cobblestone sidewalks. Jack-o'-lanterns grinned from every porch, their flickering light casting eerie shadows.

Morty stepped out of The Ghoulish Gourmet, inhaling deeply. "Ah, the sweet smell of impending doom," he mused, adjusting his chef's hat.

A group of children ran past, giggling and waving plastic fangs. Morty waved back, his smile genuine.

"This year's festival is going to be killer," he thought, chuckling at his own pun.

As he rounded the corner, he spotted a familiar figure in an ostentatious orange suit. Mayor Candy Corn stood in a shadowy alley, speaking in hushed tones with a man Morty didn't recognize.

"Now, now, let's not be hasty," the Mayor's oily voice carried. "I'm sure we can come to a mutually beneficial arrangement."

The stranger grunted, then nodded, slipping an envelope into the Mayor's jacket.

Morty frowned. Something about the exchange felt off, but he couldn't quite put his finger on it.

Mayor Candy Corn emerged from the alley, his trademark smirk firmly in place. "Ah, Mortimer! Just the man I wanted to see."

Morty plastered on a smile. "Mayor Candy Corn, always a pleasure. Excited for the festival?"

"Oh, absolutely," the Mayor replied, his voice smooth as melted chocolate. "I have a feeling this year's event will be unforgettable."

Morty couldn't shake the feeling that there was more to the Mayor's words than met the eye.

As Morty pondered the Mayor's cryptic statement, a hush fell over the bustling street. Heads turned, whispers erupted, and the crowd parted like a supernatural sea.

Willow Shadowmoon glided into view, her flowing robes shimmering with an otherworldly iridescence. Her violet eyes seemed to pierce through the very fabric of reality.

"The veil grows thin," Willow intoned, her voice soft yet carrying effortlessly. "I sense... a gathering of energies."

Morty raised an eyebrow. "Energies, huh? Hope they're the good kind."

Willow fixed her gaze on him. "The spirits whisper of change, Mortimer Graves. Your culinary creations may play a pivotal role in the cosmic dance to come."

"Well, as long as they're not complaining about my seasoning," Morty quipped, trying to hide his unease.

A few onlookers chuckled nervously, clearly enthralled by Willow's presence.

"The festival approaches," Willow continued, her words laden with portent. "Prepare yourselves for revelations most profound."

As the crowd murmured in excitement, Morty noticed a tall, striking woman observing the scene from the shadows. Dr. Frankie Stein, he realized, recognizing her silver-streaked hair and dark green eyes.

"Quite the performance," Dr. Stein remarked dryly, stepping forward. "Though I suspect our dear psychic may be overlooking some rather mundane, yet crucial details."

Morty turned his attention back to the gathering crowd, his mind whirring with culinary possibilities. He clapped his hands, a mischievous grin spreading across his face.

"Speaking of revelations, folks, wait till you see what's cooking at The Ghoulish Gourmet!"

He gestured dramatically towards his restaurant's window display. A blood-red velvet heart cake sat center stage, its fondant arteries pulsing with an eerie, lifelike quality.

"Behold, our 'Heartfelt Delight'!" Morty proclaimed. "Each slice guaranteed to make your taste buds skip a beat!"

A collective gasp rose from the onlookers. Morty's grin widened.

"And that's not all," he continued, pointing to a platter of incredibly realistic witch's finger cookies. "Try our 'Digit Delicacies' – don't worry, no witches were harmed in the making!"

An elderly woman peered closer. "Goodness, they look so real!"

Morty winked. "The secret's in the almond slivers, ma'am. Makes for the perfect gnarly nail!"

He watched as curiosity overcame initial hesitation. The crowd pressed closer, eager for more details.

"What else you got cooking, Morty?" someone called out.

Morty's eyes gleamed with excitement. This was his moment to shine.

The streets of Hollow Creek buzzed with anticipation. Orange and black streamers fluttered from lampposts. Carved pumpkins grinned from every doorstep. The air smelled of cinnamon and wood smoke.

Morty stepped out of The Ghoulish Gourmet, his chef's hat bobbing as he surveyed the scene. A grin spread across his face.

"Well, if it isn't a graveyard smash out here!" he called out to passing neighbors.

Mrs. Thornberry, struggling with an armful of fake cobwebs, stumbled nearby. Morty rushed to steady her.

"Careful there, Mrs. T! Wouldn't want you to get caught in your own web of deceit," he chuckled, helping untangle her.

She rolled her eyes but smiled. "Oh Morty, your puns are worse than your cooking."

"I'll take that as a compliment!" He winked. "Speaking of which, care for a 'Boo-berry' muffin? They're to die for!"

Morty produced a pastry from his apron pocket. Mrs. Thornberry eyed it suspiciously.

"It's not actually moldy, is it?" she asked.

"Only in color, I assure you. The secret's all in the food dye!"

As Mrs. Thornberry took a tentative bite, Morty's mind raced with ideas for his festival menu. He'd need something truly spectacular to outdo last year's 'Frankenstein's Monster Mash Potatoes'.

"By the pricking of my thumbs, something wicked this way comes," he muttered to himself, grinning at the possibilities.

A sleek black sedan rolled down Main Street, its tinted windows reflecting the festive decorations. The car slowed to a stop, and out stepped Mayor Candy Corn, his autumnal suit clashing garishly with the Halloween decor.

"My dear constituents!" he called out, his voice dripping with false warmth. "How delightful to see you all embracing the spirit of the season!"

Morty watched as the mayor glad-handed his way through the crowd. His eyes narrowed.

"That man could charm the fangs off a vampire," Morty muttered under his breath.

Mayor Candy Corn spotted Morty and made a beeline for him. "Ah, Mr. Graves! I trust your culinary creations will be the highlight of our upcoming festivities?"

"You bet your candy corn, Mr. Mayor," Morty replied, forcing a smile. "Though I hope you're not planning another 'surprise health inspection' like last year."

The mayor's laugh was as hollow as a jack-o'-lantern. "Now, now, my good man. Those inspections are for the greater good of Hollow Creek. We wouldn't want any... unfortunate incidents, would we?"

Morty felt a chill that had nothing to do with the autumn air. Before he could respond, a hush fell over the street.

Willow Shadowmoon glided through the crowd, her violet eyes seeming to glow in the fading light. She stopped before Morty and the mayor, her gaze piercing.

"The veil grows thin," she intoned, her voice soft yet commanding. "I sense a darkness looming, a shadow cast by greed and deceit."

Mayor Candy Corn's smile faltered for a moment. "Miss Shadowmoon, always a pleasure. Though perhaps we could tone down the doom and gloom? This is a celebration, after all!"

As the tension thickened like congealing blood pudding, a new voice cut through the air, cool and precise.

"Interesting hypothesis, Miss Shadowmoon. Though I'd posit that darkness is simply the absence of light, not an entity unto itself."

Morty turned to see a tall, striking woman with jet-black hair streaked with silver. Dr. Frankie Stein. She scanned the group with a hint of amusement.

"Dr. Stein," Morty said, relief evident in his voice. "Care to weigh in on our little... disagreement?"

"I prefer to observe rather than intervene, Mr. Graves," she replied, her tone measured. "Though I must say, your 'Zombie Brain Pâté' has piqued my scientific curiosity. The texture is remarkably authentic."

Morty grinned, momentarily forgetting the tense atmosphere. "Trade secret, Doc. But I'd be happy to give you a behind-the-scenes tour of The Ghoulish Gourmet sometime."

"Perhaps," Dr. Stein said, a ghost of a smile on her lips. "I find that kitchens and laboratories often share more similarities than one might expect."

The mayor, sensing he was losing control of the conversation, cleared his throat. "Speaking of The Ghoulish Gourmet, I hear it's quite the hotspot these days, Morty. Care to elaborate?"

Morty's eyes lit up. "Oh, you should see the line stretching down Mummy Lane! Folks can't get enough of our Bat Wing Bruschetta and Eyeball Soup. It's to die for – figuratively speaking, of course."

Morty's excitement bubbled over as he surveyed his bustling restaurant. The Ghoulish Gourmet was packed, patrons eagerly devouring his latest creations. He grinned, his wild hair seeming to crackle with electric energy.

"Just wait till they see what I've cooked up for the festival," he mused, rubbing his hands together.

A server rushed by, balancing a tray of Mummy Meatloaf. "Chef! Table 13 wants to know if the bandages are edible!"

Morty chuckled. "Tell them everything's edible if you're brave enough!"

He turned back to his kitchen, mind racing with possibilities. The Halloween Festival was his chance to truly shine, to cement his legacy in culinary infamy.

"This year," he muttered, "I'll knock their socks off. Maybe literally, if I get that Sock-It-To-Me Punch recipe right."

As he reached for his recipe book, a chill ran down his spine. The lights flickered ominously. Morty froze, wooden spoon in hand.

"What in the name of Julia Child's ghost...?" he whispered.

Suddenly, the kitchen plunged into darkness. A blood-curdling scream echoed from the dining room.

Best Served Dead

Morty grabbed the handle to the walk in freezer. Darkness swallowed him. He grabbed at the cord on the side of the door where a flashlight hung and grabbed it. He pressed the switch and shined the light inside the freezer. He felt the blood drain from his face and air solidify in his throat.

There, sprawled on the floor, was Ima Picky. Her lifeless eyes stared blankly upward. Her fingers clutched a tub of his prized pumpkin ice cream.

Morty's mind raced. This couldn't be happening. Not in his restaurant. Not to his nemesis-turned-almost-ally.

He opened his mouth to call for help, but no sound came out.

Footsteps approached behind him. "Chef, did you find the dry ice? We need more for the smoking cauldron coc—oh my god!"

Bella pushed past him into the freezer. Her eyes went wide as saucers. She pointed a trembling finger at Ima's body.

"I-I didn't... I just came for dry ice!" Bella stammered. "I had nothing to do with this!"

Morty finally found his voice. "Neither did I, Bella. But who would want Ima dead?"

"Maybe someone who got a bad review?" Bella suggested weakly.

Morty shook his head. "Half the chefs in town would be suspects then."

He stared at the tub of ice cream in Ima's grasp. His secret recipe. The one she'd threatened to expose.

A chill ran down his spine that had nothing to do with the freezer.

The sound of sirens pierced the air, growing louder by the second. Morty's heart raced as he heard heavy footsteps approaching the freezer.

Detective Jack O'Lantern burst through the door, his tie askew and his hair more disheveled than usual. His eyes widened comically as he took in the grim scene.

"Great pumpkins!" Jack exclaimed. "Looks like someone's gotten themselves into a pickle... or should I say, a popsicle?"

He crouched down, examining Ima's body and the tub of ice cream she clutched. "Hmm, death by dessert. That's a new one."

Morty's stomach churned. He needed to explain, to defend himself. "Detective, I swear I had nothing to do with this! I just found her like this when I came for dry ice."

Jack raised an eyebrow. "Dry ice, eh? Sounds like a cold-blooded alibi to me."

"No, no, you don't understand," Morty stammered, his usual wit deserting him. "Ima and I, we were just starting to get along. Why would I hurt her?"

The detective stood, brushing imaginary dust from his wrinkled pants. "Well, Mr. Graves, sometimes the sweetest treats hide the bitterest secrets. Care to explain why the victim is holding your famous ice cream like it's her last lifeline?"

Morty's mind raced. How could he explain without revealing his secret recipe? "I... I don't know. Maybe she just really liked it?"

Jack's eyes narrowed. "Or maybe she discovered something about it she wasn't supposed to know."

Morty swallowed hard, his dark humor bubbling up despite the gravity of the situation. "Well, Detective, I always said my ice cream was to die for, but this is ridiculous."

Jack shot him a disapproving look. "This is no time for jokes, Mr. Graves. We've got a real chilling situation on our hands."

The portly chef watched as Jack fumbled with a pair of latex gloves, struggling to put them on his large hands. Morty's mind whirled with possibilities. Who could have done this? And why use his ice cream?

"Detective," Morty ventured, "you might want to check the freezer door. It's got a tricky lock. Maybe there are fingerprints?"

Jack's eyes lit up. "Ah-ha! Good thinking, Mr. Graves. I was just about to do that myself."

As the detective examined the door, Morty's gaze drifted back to Ima's body. Her fingers were practically fused to the ice cream container. He couldn't help but quip, "Looks like she got a real brain freeze, eh?"

Jack spun around, nearly losing his balance. "Mr. Graves! This is a murder investigation, not an open mic night at the Crypt Cafe!"

Morty raised his hands in surrender. "Sorry, sorry. It's just... well, you have to admit, it's pretty ironic. Ima Picky, the harshest food critic in Hollow Creek, found dead clutching my pumpkin ice cream. It's like a twisted endorsement. Gives a whole new meaning to *"Will cost you an arm and a leg."*

Bella's trembling hands smoothed her chef's coat as she approached Detective O'Lantern. Her voice quivered, barely above a whisper. "Detective, I... I want to help. Morty didn't do this."

Jack squinted at her, his tie askew. "And how can you be so sure, Miss...?"

"Notte. Bella Notte," she replied, her voice steadying. "I was with Morty all evening. We were prepping for tomorrow's Halloween special."

Jack's eyebrows shot up. "A Halloween special? In a place called The Ghoulish Gourmet? Isn't that a bit... on the nose?"

Bella blinked, confused. "I... I don't understand."

"Never mind," Jack muttered. "Tell me what happened."

As Bella recounted the evening's events, Morty paced nearby, his wild hair seeming to crackle with nervous energy. He couldn't help but interject.

"Detective, I swear on my grandmother's grave - which, by the way, makes an excellent backdrop for our annual Zombie Zucchini bread photoshoot - that I had nothing to do with this."

Jack held up a hand. "Mr. Graves, please. I need to interview you both separately. Miss Notte, if you'll come with me."

As they walked away, Morty called out, "Bella, remember - the truth will set you free... unlike poor Ima in there!"

Jack groaned. "Mr. Graves, one more quip and I'll have to put you on ice."

Morty's face fell, his usual jovial demeanor cracking under the weight of the situation. He tugged at his spooky apron, fingers tracing the outline of a grinning jack-o'-lantern. His mind raced.

"Detective," he began, his voice uncharacteristically solemn. "I've dedicated my life to this restaurant. To Hollow Creek. Why would I jeopardize that?"

Jack's stern gaze softened slightly. "I understand, Mr. Graves. But I need facts, not sentiment."

Morty nodded, swallowing hard. "Of course. Ask away."

As Jack questioned him, Morty's eyes kept darting to the freezer. He shuddered, remembering Ima's lifeless form.

Meanwhile, Bella sat across from another officer, wringing her hands. "Morty's been nothing but kind to me," she insisted, her voice trembling. "He took me in when no other chef would. He's... he's like family."

The officer leaned forward. "Did you notice anything unusual about Ms. Picky's behavior tonight?"

Bella shook her head, then paused. "Well... she did seem more critical than usual. But that's just Ima being Ima, right?"

Back with Morty, Jack was pressing harder. "Mr. Graves, your prints are all over that ice cream tub. Care to explain?"

Morty's eyes widened. "Well, I should hope so! I made the ice cream, after all. It's my To Die For Petrifying Pumpkin Swirl." He winced at his poor choice of words.

Jack's brow furrowed. He pulled on a pair of latex gloves and carefully lifted the ice cream tub. "We'll need to examine this more closely," he muttered.

Morty's heart raced. His legendary pumpkin ice cream, now evidence in a murder investigation. The irony wasn't lost on him.

"Detective, that recipe is a family secret," Morty protested weakly.

Jack raised an eyebrow. "Mr. Graves, we have a dead food critic. Your secret recipe is the least of our concerns."

Bella, overhearing, chimed in. "But Detective, Morty's ice cream is what makes The Ghoulish Gourmet special!"

Jack sighed. "Miss Notte, Mr. Graves, I need you both to remain here while we process the scene. Don't leave the premises."

As Jack walked away, Morty's mind whirled. He had to do something. He couldn't let his reputation – or his freedom – melt away like a scoop of ice cream in the summer sun.

"Bella," he whispered, "we need to find out who really did this."

Bella's eyes widened. "But how? We're not detectives."

Morty's lips curled into a grim smile. "No, but we know this town. And its secrets."

Morty glanced around, ensuring Detective Jack was out of earshot. "Listen, Bella. We need to start digging. Who had it out for Ima?"

Bella fidgeted with her apron. "Well, half the restaurateurs in town, for starters. Her reviews were brutal."

"Exactly," Morty nodded, his wild hair bobbing. "We need to make a list."

As they huddled together, whispering names, a commotion erupted near the freezer. Officer Candy Corn, Jack's bumbling deputy, had tripped over an evidence marker.

"Great ghostly gnocchi!" Morty exclaimed. "That man's clumsier than a zombie in a china shop."

Bella stifled a giggle, then sobered. "Morty, what if we get caught snooping?"

Morty's eyes twinkled mischievously. "Then we'll just have to use our noodles, won't we? And I don't mean the pasta kind."

Suddenly, Jack's voice boomed across the kitchen. "Mr. Graves! A word, please."

Morty's heart skipped a beat. Had Jack overheard their plotting? He squeezed Bella's shoulder reassuringly and shuffled towards the detective.

"Coming, Detective! Just trying to digest this chilling situation," Morty called out, his voice wavering slightly.

As Morty approached, Jack's stern expression sent a shiver down his spine. What had the detective uncovered?

CHAPTER 2

Morty's mind churned like a cauldron of boiling broth. The cold steel bars of his cell bit into his palms as he gripped them tightly. He couldn't shake the image of Ima Picky's frozen corpse from his thoughts.

"I didn't do it," he muttered to himself. "And I'll prove it, or my name isn't Mortimer Graves."

He paced the small cell, his chef's clogs clicking against the concrete floor. The familiar weight of his apron was missing, replaced by the scratchy fabric of a prison jumpsuit.

"Think, Morty, think," he urged himself. "There's got to be a clue you're missing."

A hushed conversation from the neighboring cell caught his attention. Morty's ears perked up like a cat sensing a mouse.

"You hear about that chef who offed the food critic?" a gruff voice asked.

"Yeah, froze her solid in his own walk-in," another replied with a chuckle. "Cold as one of his ice cream scoops."

Morty's heart skipped a beat. He inched closer to the wall, straining to hear more.

"But get this," the first voice continued. "I heard it might not have been him at all. Could've been his sous chef."

"No kidding? Why her?"

"Name's Bella something. Italian, I think. She had access to the freezer too. Plus, word is she's got ambition. Maybe wanted the big job for herself."

Morty's eyes widened. Bella? His loyal, timid Bella? It couldn't be. Could it?

He opened his mouth to interject, to defend his protégé. But something held him back. A nagging doubt, small as a grain of salt, had been planted.

Morty slumped onto his cot, his mind reeling. He'd teach Bella everything he knew. She was like family. But as the saying went, you can't pick your family - or always trust them.

"Oh, Bella," he sighed. "What have you gotten yourself into?"

Morty cleared his throat, his voice carrying a forced lightness. "Couldn't help but overhear, gents. This Bella character sounds intriguing. Care to share more?"

A beat of silence followed. Then, a face appeared at the bars of the neighboring cell. "Well, well. If it ain't the Ghoulish Gourmet himself. Fishing for info, are we?"

Morty shrugged, his chains clinking. "Just trying to make sense of this mess. Bella's my sous chef, you see."

The inmate's eyebrows shot up. "No kidding? Well, ain't that something."

Before Morty could probe further, a new voice chimed in from across the hall. "Bella Notte? That sweet little thing? Nah, you've got it all wrong."

Morty's head snapped towards the source. A lanky man with disheveled hair leaned against his cell bars. "Name's Teddy. Used to work for Ima Picky. Trust me, if anyone had reason to want that woman gone, it wasn't your Bella."

Morty's curiosity piqued. "Oh? Do tell, Teddy."

Teddy's face darkened. "Ima was a nightmare. Treated her assistants like dirt. I lasted three months before I quit. But Bella? She catered an event for Ima once. Poor girl was in tears by the end of it."

Morty's stomach churned. He'd never known about that incident. What else had Bella kept from him?

Morty's mind raced. He needed more information, and these inmates seemed to be a goldmine. He leaned forward, his voice dropping to a conspiratorial whisper. "Gentlemen, I'm all ears. Anything else you can tell me about Ima's... connections?"

Teddy glanced around nervously before speaking. "Well, there's one thing. Ima and Mayor Candy Corn were thick as thieves."

Morty's eyebrows shot up. "The mayor? Now that's interesting."

A stocky inmate in the corner chuckled. "Interesting? Try scandalous. Candy Corn's been in Ima's pocket for years."

Morty's mind whirled. Could the mayor be involved? He pressed on, his tone casual. "How so?"

Teddy leaned closer. "Ima had dirt on him. Threatened to expose some shady deals if he didn't play ball. Her reviews could make or break businesses in this town."

The stocky inmate nodded. "Word is, Candy Corn was getting tired of dancing to her tune. A bad review could've tanked his re-election chances."

Morty felt a chill run down his spine. "So, the mayor had motive?"

Teddy shrugged. "Motive, means, and one hell of a sweet tooth for power."

Morty's thoughts raced. The mayor, a potential murderer? It seemed far-fetched, yet... He needed to dig deeper.

Morty's mind reeled. Mayor Candy Corn, Bella, and now who else? He leaned against the cold cell wall, his brow furrowed in concentration.

"Seems like our dear Ima had quite a few enemies," Morty mused aloud, his voice tinged with dark humor. "Any other skeletons rattling in her closet?"

The stocky inmate, who'd introduced himself as Buster, let out a dry chuckle. "You kidding? That woman collected enemies like Halloween candy."

Morty's ears perked up. He needed to steer the conversation subtly. "Speaking of Halloween, I heard Ima wasn't too fond of our local psychic. What was her name again?"

"Willow Shadowmoon," Teddy supplied, rolling his eyes. "That kooky fortune-teller down on Specter Street."

Morty feigned surprise. "Oh? What's the story there?"

Buster snorted. "Ima thought Willow was a total fraud. Called her out in public more than once."

"Really now?" Morty prompted, his interest genuine.

Teddy nodded vigorously. "Oh yeah. I was there for one of their showdowns. Ima tore into Willow something fierce, called her a 'charlatan' and a 'disgrace to Hollow Creek.'"

Morty winced. "Ouch. How'd Willow take that?"

"Not well," Buster said, lowering his voice. "I saw her later that night, muttering some weird incantations. Said she was gonna 'show Ima the true power of the spirit world.'"

Morty's eyes widened. Could Willow have...? No, surely not. But then again, in this town, anything was possible.

Morty's mind raced. He glanced at the small window in his cell, noticing the waning moon. Halloween was approaching fast. Time was slipping away like sand through an hourglass.

"Blast it all," he muttered, running a hand through his wild hair. "I need more than just gossip and hearsay."

Buster leaned in, his voice low. "What's eating you, chef?"

Morty sighed, his usual jovial demeanor faltering. "If I don't clear my name soon, The Ghoulish Gourmet will be nothing but a ghost story."

An idea struck him like lightning. He turned to his fellow inmates, a mischievous glint in his eye. "Say, fellas, you wouldn't happen to know anyone else who had a bone to pick with our dearly departed critic?"

Teddy scratched his chin. "Well, there was that health inspector she got fired last year..."

Morty's ears perked up. "Oh? Do tell."

"Guy named Frank Furter," Buster chimed in. "Ima caught him taking bribes from some sketchy food truck operators."

Morty leaned forward, his curiosity piqued. "And how did our friend Frank feel about that?"

Teddy snickered. "Let's just say he wasn't exactly singing Ima's praises. Last I heard, he was working as a janitor at the Hollow Creek Community Center."

Morty filed away this information, his mind already formulating a plan. He'd need to get creative to dig deeper into these potential suspects.

"Gentlemen," he said, a sly grin spreading across his face, "I believe it's time we stirred up some trouble in this cauldron of ours."

Morty's eyes gleamed with mischief. He rubbed his hands together, a plan bubbling in his mind like a witch's brew.

"How about I whip up a little Halloween treat for you boys?" he offered, his voice low and enticing.

Buster's eyebrows shot up. "In here? How?"

Morty winked. "A chef never reveals his secrets. But let's just say I can make magic with what's available."

He set to work, using his tray as a makeshift cutting board. With deft hands, he transformed bland prison fare into something extraordinary.

"Behold," Morty announced dramatically, "my Jailhouse Jack-o'-Lantern Surprise!"

The inmates gathered, eyes wide with curiosity. Morty's creation was a grotesque yet oddly appetizing face made from mashed potatoes, with carrot strips for hair and olive slices for eyes.

"Looks spooky," Teddy muttered, but his stomach growled.

As they dug in, Morty regaled them with tales of his most outrageous culinary experiments. The cell block filled with laughter and excited chatter.

"So," Morty said casually, "any of you boys ever cross paths with Willow Shadowmoon?"

Buster snorted. "That fraud? Ima tore her act to shreds in one of her reviews."

Morty leaned in, his interest piqued. "Oh? Do tell."

Morty's mind whirred like a food processor, dicing and blending the information he'd gathered. He paced his cell, each step bringing clarity.

"Bella had access, but Willow had motive," he muttered. "And the mayor... what's his angle?"

He turned to Buster, who was licking the last bits of potato from his fingers. "Say, wasn't there some scandal with Mayor Candy Corn last year?"

Buster's eyes narrowed. "Yeah, somethin' about missin' funds. Ima was sniffin' around that story."

Morty's eyebrows shot up. "Well, butter my biscuits! That's quite the tidbit."

A guard's voice boomed down the corridor. "Lights out in five, fellas!"

Morty felt a surge of urgency. He needed more time, more information. But the cell doors were closing in on his investigation.

"Listen," he whispered to his cellmates. "I need your help. My restaurant's on the chopping block if I don't solve this soon."

Best Served Dead

Teddy leaned in. "What's in it for us, Chef?"

Morty's mind raced. "How about a lifetime supply of my famous Bone-Chilling Brownies once I'm out?"

The inmates exchanged glances, then nodded eagerly.

As darkness fell, Morty lay on his bunk, his resolve hardening like caramel in cold water. He'd crack this case, no matter the obstacles. His restaurant, his legacy, depended on it.

Morty sat up abruptly, his wild hair even more disheveled than usual. A plan was taking shape in his mind, as intricate as one of his Halloween-themed pastry designs.

"Alright, my ghoulish gourmands," he whispered to his cellmates. "Here's what we're going to do."

Buster and Teddy leaned in, their eyes glinting with curiosity.

"We need to create a distraction," Morty explained, his voice low and excited. "Something to get the guards' attention while I make a few... strategic phone calls."

Teddy raised an eyebrow. "What kind of distraction we talkin' about, Chef?"

Morty's lips curled into a mischievous grin. "How about a little culinary chaos? I'll need your help to stage a food fight during tomorrow's lunch."

Buster chuckled. "Now that's what I call a tasty plan."

As they huddled closer, Morty outlined the details of his scheme. His hands moved animatedly, as if he were conducting an orchestra of mischief.

"Once the coast is clear, I'll sweet-talk my way to the phone. We'll need to time it perfectly."

Just then, a guard's flashlight beam swept across their cell. Morty froze mid-gesture, his heart pounding like a chef's knife on a cutting board.

"Lights out means lights out, Graves," the guard growled.

As the light moved on, Morty let out a relieved sigh. He settled back onto his bunk, mind racing with possibilities and potential pitfalls.

Tomorrow would be crucial. If his plan worked, he'd be one step closer to clearing his name. If it failed...

Morty pushed the thought away. Failure wasn't an option. Not when The Ghoulish Gourmet's fate hung in the balance.

As he drifted off to sleep, visions of suspect interrogations danced in his head. He'd get to the bottom of this mystery, one way or another.

Little did Morty know, as he plotted his next move, that someone else was making plans of their own. Plans that could turn his world upside down faster than a poorly executed soufflé.

CHAPTER 3

The cot creaked as Morty shifted his weight. Steel bars cast long shadows across the cramped cell. He sprang up, pacing the confined space like a caged animal.

"Blasted pumpkin-headed buffoons," Morty muttered, running a hand through his wild hair. "I'll clear my name faster than you can say 'boo.' The Ghoulish Gourmet won't go down without a fight."

His stomach growled. Morty longed for his kitchen—the simmering cauldrons, the bubbling brews. Instead, he was stuck here with nothing but his thoughts and the faint smell of mildew.

The cell door creaked open. Morty whirled around, hope flaring in his chest. It deflated when he saw it wasn't his lawyer.

A tall woman glided into the cell. Her presence filled the small space, commanding attention without uttering a word. She surveyed the scene, taking in every detail.

Morty froze mid-step. "Who are you?" he asked, curiosity overriding his initial disappointment.

The woman's gaze locked onto Morty. A slight smile played at the corners of her mouth. "Dr. Frankie Stein," she said, her voice smooth and controlled. "I believe we have much to discuss, Mr. Graves."

Morty's eyebrows shot up. He'd heard whispers about this mysterious woman. What could she want with him?

Morty crossed his arms, eyeing Dr. Frankie Stein warily. His bushy eyebrows knitted together, skepticism etched on his face. What game was she playing?

"Much to discuss?" Morty scoffed. "Unless you're here to whip up an alibi soufflé, I don't see how you can help."

Dr. Stein's smile didn't waver. She took a step closer, her dark garments swishing softly. "I assure you, Mr. Graves, my expertise goes far beyond the culinary realm."

Morty's eyes narrowed. "Oh? And what exactly is your area of expertise, Doctor?"

"I specialize in arcane sciences and mystical arts," she replied, her tone matter-of-fact. "Skills that could prove quite useful in unraveling your current... predicament."

Morty barked out a laugh. "Arcane sciences? Mystical arts? What is this, a Halloween party trick?"

Dr. Stein's gaze never wavered. "I assure you, Mr. Graves, my abilities are far from tricks. They've helped solve cases that left conventional methods baffled."

Morty's skepticism warred with his desperation. He needed help, but could he trust this enigmatic woman?

"And why, pray tell, would you want to help me?" he asked, unable to keep the suspicion from his voice.

Dr. Stein's lips curved into a knowing smile. "Let's just say I have a vested interest in uncovering the truth. Hollow Creek thrives on its mysteries, but some secrets are better brought to light."

Morty leaned forward, his curiosity piqued despite himself. "And how exactly would your... unconventional methods help clear my name?"

"I can see beyond the surface, Mr. Graves," Dr. Stein explained, her voice low and compelling. "Trace the threads of motive and opportunity that others might miss. Uncover the hidden truths that lie beneath the obvious facts."

Morty's mind raced. Could this be the break he needed? He scratched his chin, considering. "And what makes you think Ima Picky's murder is anything more than a simple case of food poisoning gone wrong?"

Dr. Stein's green eyes glinted. "Because, Mr. Graves, nothing in Hollow Creek is ever simple. Especially not when it comes to death."

She extended her hand, pale and slender. "Allow me to assist you. Together, we can navigate this web of suspects and motives. What do you say?"

Morty stared at her outstretched hand, torn between hope and suspicion. Could he trust her? Did he have a choice?

Morty's fingers twitched, hovering inches from Dr. Stein's extended hand. His brow furrowed as he scratched his chin, wild hair crackling with static electricity.

"I don't know," he muttered, more to himself than to her. "This all seems a bit... far-fetched."

Dr. Stein remained motionless, her piercing green eyes locked on Morty's face. She exuded an air of patience, as if she had all the time in the world.

Morty paced the small cell, his chef's apron adorned with tiny grinning pumpkins swishing with each step. "Look, Doc," he said, gesturing wildly, "I appreciate the offer, but how do I know you're not just another kook looking for their fifteen minutes of fame?"

A hint of amusement flickered across Dr. Stein's face. "Mr. Graves, if fame were my goal, I assure you there are far more lucrative avenues than assisting an accused murderer."

Morty stopped pacing, eyeing her warily. "Fair point. But still, arcane sciences? Mystical arts? Sounds like something out of a B-movie."

"Says the man who claims his pumpkin ice cream has supernatural properties," Dr. Stein countered, one eyebrow raised.

Morty couldn't help but chuckle. "Touché, Doc. Touché."

Morty's laughter faded, replaced by a steely resolve. He straightened his spine, a determined glint in his eyes. With a slow, deliberate nod, he reached out and clasped Dr. Stein's hand.

"Alright, Doc. You've got yourself a deal," Morty said, his voice gravelly with emotion. "Let's clear my name and save The Ghoulish Gourmet."

Dr. Stein's lips curved into a satisfied smile. "Excellent choice, Mr. Graves."

Without missing a beat, she withdrew her hand and reached into a sleek leather satchel. Out came a weathered notebook and an ornate silver pen that seemed to glow faintly in the dim cell light.

"Now," Dr. Stein said, flipping open the notebook, "let's review what we know about Ms. Picky's demise."

Morty leaned against the cell bars, arms crossed. "Not much to tell. One minute she's tearing my blood pudding soufflé to shreds, the next she's face-down in it."

Dr. Stein's pen scratched across the paper. "Interesting. And the cause of death?"

"Poison, they said. In the soufflé." Morty's face darkened. "Which is ridiculous. I may have wanted to shut her up, but I'd never poison my own food. It's sacrilege!"

"Hmm," Dr. Stein murmured, jotting more notes. "And the other diners?"

Morty shrugged. "The usual Halloween crowd. Witches, vampires, one particularly convincing zombie."

Dr. Stein's eyes narrowed. "Costumes, I presume?"

"In Hollow Creek? You never know," Morty replied with a wry grin.

Dr. Stein tapped her pen against her chin. "Interesting indeed. Tell me, Mr. Graves, did Ms. Picky have any known enemies?"

Morty snorted. "Besides every chef in town? The woman was a menace with a fork and a poison pen."

He leaned closer, watching as Dr. Stein sketched a web of names and arrows. Her handwriting was precise, almost architectural in its neatness.

"There was that incident with Bella Donna's Botanical Bistro last month," Morty offered. "Ima claimed their 'all-natural' menu was laced with artificial preservatives. Nearly shut them down."

Dr. Stein's eyebrow arched. "Potential motive. Go on."

Morty scratched his stubbled chin. "And let's not forget Vlad's Plasma Palace. Ima exposed their 'blood' smoothies as nothing more than beet juice with food coloring."

"Fascinating," Dr. Stein murmured, adding more lines to her diagram. "It seems Ms. Picky had quite the talent for making enemies."

Morty nodded vigorously. "You're telling me. Half the town wanted her silenced. Just not, you know, permanently."

Dr. Stein's pen paused. She fixed Morty with a penetrating gaze. "And what about you, Mr. Graves? What was your relationship with the victim?"

Morty's stomach churned. He swallowed hard. "Me? I, uh... well, let's just say we had a complicated history."

Morty's skepticism melted away as he watched Dr. Stein work. Her methodical approach and razor-sharp insights were undeniable. He found himself nodding along, a newfound trust blossoming between them.

"You know," Morty mused, "I never thought I'd say this, but you might actually be onto something here, Doc."

Dr. Stein's lips quirked in a half-smile. "I appreciate your vote of confidence, Mr. Graves."

Morty leaned back against the cold cell wall, his mind whirring. "So, if we follow this thread about Bella Donna's revenge plot..."

"Indeed," Dr. Stein interjected, "it could lead us to a rather poisonous conclusion."

Morty chuckled, despite himself. "Was that a pun, Doc? I'm impressed."

Dr. Stein's eyes twinkled. "I do try to keep up with the local color."

As they continued to piece together the puzzle, Morty felt a weight lifting from his shoulders. For the first time since his arrest, hope flickered in his chest.

"Dr. Stein," he said, his voice thick with emotion, "I can't thank you enough for your help. Without you, I'd still be stirring in my own juices, going nowhere fast."

Dr. Stein nodded graciously. "Your insights have been invaluable, Mr. Graves. This partnership has proven quite fruitful."

Morty straightened up, determination etched on his face. "You can count on my full cooperation moving forward. Whatever it takes to clear my name and save The Ghoulish Gourmet."

As Morty opened his mouth to speak again, a loud crash echoed through the jail. The cell door flew open, revealing Detective Jack O'Lantern, his tie askew and eyes wild.

"Graves! You've got a visitor," Jack announced, stumbling over his words. "I mean, another one. A real live wire!"

Morty raised an eyebrow. "Who could that be? My dance card's already full with the good doctor here."

Dr. Stein stood, smoothing her lab coat. "Perhaps it's someone with new information?"

Jack scratched his head. "Uh, yeah. Information. That's what she said. Something about a 'smoking bun'?"

Morty's eyes widened. "Smoking bun? That sounds like-"

"Bella!" they exclaimed in unison.

As if on cue, Bella Notte appeared behind Jack, her chef's coat dusted with flour and her eyes brimming with tears.

"Chef Morty!" she cried. "I've got something that might help, but-"

Suddenly, the lights flickered and went out. In the darkness, a scream pierced the air, followed by the sound of running footsteps.

Morty's heart raced. "Bella? Doc? Anyone?"

The lights snapped back on, revealing an empty doorway. Bella was gone.

CHAPTER 4

Morty burst into Mayor Candy Corn's office, the door slamming against the wall with a thunderous crack. The scent of pumpkin spice air freshener mingled with the mayor's cloying cologne, making Morty's nose wrinkle.

"What's the meaning of this, Mayor?" Morty demanded, his wild hair crackling with static electricity. "Why are you trying to shut down my restaurant?"

Mayor Candy Corn's perpetual smirk widened as he leaned back in his leather chair. "Now, now, Mortimer. Let's not jump to conclusions."

Morty's eyes narrowed. This slippery politician wasn't going to weasel his way out of this one.

"Cut the act," Morty growled. "I know you're behind the health code violations and the rumors about my food."

The mayor steepled his fingers, his candy corn cufflinks glinting in the fluorescent light. "I assure you, I have no idea what you're talking about."

Morty slammed his hands on the desk, rattling the mayor's name plaque. "Don't play dumb with me, Cornelius. I want answers!"

Mayor Candy Corn's oily smile never faltered. "I'm simply looking out for our beloved Hollow Creek. The Halloween Festival is approaching, and we can't have any... unsavory incidents."

Morty's mind raced. The festival. Of course. The mayor was worried about his precious reputation.

"My restaurant has been a staple of this town for years," Morty countered. "You can't just shut it down on a whim!"

The mayor's eyes glinted dangerously. "Oh, but I can, Mortimer. I can do a lot of things."

Morty felt a chill run down his spine. This confrontation was far from over.

Morty's fists clenched at his sides. He wouldn't let this pompous candy corn scare him off.

"You're risking the livelihood of my staff and disappointing our loyal customers," Morty said, his voice low and intense. "All to protect your precious political career."

Mayor Candy Corn's smirk faltered for a split second. "Watch your tone, Graves. You're treading on thin ice."

Morty leaned in closer, the scent of cheap cologne assaulting his nostrils. "No, you're the one on thin ice. I won't stand by while you abuse your power."

The mayor's face reddened, clashing with his garish orange tie. "You have no proof of any wrongdoing."

"Not yet," Morty shot back, "but I will. And when I do, this town will see you for the fraud you are."

Mayor Candy Corn stood abruptly, his chair scraping against the floor. "You're making a grave mistake, Mortimer."

Morty didn't flinch. "The only mistake was letting you run this town for so long."

The tension in the room was palpable, crackling like the static in Morty's wild hair. Neither man was willing to back down.

Mayor Candy Corn's eyes narrowed to slits. He leaned across his desk, his voice dropping to a menacing whisper. "Let me make this crystal clear, Graves. If you persist with this foolish investigation, you might find your beloved Ghoulish Gourmet facing some... unexpected challenges."

Morty's heart raced, but he kept his face impassive. He wouldn't give this corrupt politician the satisfaction of seeing him rattled.

"Health inspections, tax audits, permit issues," the mayor continued, ticking off each threat on his pudgy fingers. "It would be a shame if your little haunted eatery became truly ghostly, wouldn't it?"

Morty's mind whirled. The restaurant was his life's work, his family's legacy. But the truth mattered more. He straightened his spine, meeting the mayor's gaze unflinchingly.

"Nice try, Candy Corn," Morty said, injecting a hint of dark humor into his voice. "But I've faced scarier things than bureaucratic bullying. Ever tried to perfect a screaming banshee soufflé?"

The mayor's smirk faltered, clearly thrown by Morty's refusal to be intimidated.

Morty pressed on, his resolve strengthening with each word. "I will uncover the truth about this murder, and any other skeletons you've got hidden in your candy-coated closet. No matter the cost."

He turned to leave, pausing at the door. "And mayor? My pumpkin ice cream will still be here long after your political career has melted away."

Mayor Candy Corn's face flushed an alarming shade of orange. He slammed his fist on the desk, sending a cascade of candy corn spilling from a nearby bowl.

"You're playing a dangerous game, Graves!" he sputtered, bits of saliva flying from his lips. "I've buried better men than you!"

Morty's eyes narrowed. He'd struck a nerve. "Buried, you say? Interesting choice of words, Mr. Mayor."

The chef reached into his apron pocket, withdrawing a crumpled newspaper clipping. He smoothed it out on the mayor's desk, revealing a faded headline: "Local Activist Vanishes, Foul Play Suspected."

"Remember Sally Specter? She was investigating city hall corruption before she mysteriously disappeared." Morty's voice was low, dangerous. "Funny how that case went cold so quickly."

Mayor Candy Corn's face drained of color. His hands trembled as he reached for the clipping.

Morty slapped his hand away. "I've got more where that came from. The Brunswick Park 'accident.' The missing funds from the Pumpkin Parade. It's all starting to add up, isn't it?"

The mayor's oily charm evaporated. "You... you can't prove anything!"

"Maybe not yet," Morty conceded, a grim smile playing on his lips. "But I'm just getting started."

Mayor Candy Corn's face contorted, his political mask slipping. He jabbed a pudgy finger at Morty. "You're the real threat to this town, Graves! Always stirring up trouble with your wild accusations and... and your ghastly food!"

Morty raised an eyebrow. "My 'Screaming Banshee Soufflé' is a local favorite, I'll have you know."

The mayor paced behind his desk, his candy corn-patterned tie swinging wildly. "You're destabilizing Hollow Creek! People are scared, businesses are suffering. And it's all because you can't let this ridiculous murder investigation go!"

Morty felt a surge of anger. He planted his hands on the mayor's desk, leaning in. "Ridiculous? Someone died, Cornelius. Or have you forgotten that in your rush to sweep it under the rug?"

Mayor Candy Corn's eyes darted nervously. "I'm thinking of the greater good. The Halloween Festival—"

"The festival can wait," Morty interrupted. "What about justice? What about the safety of our town?"

The chef straightened up, his resolve strengthening. "I've been serving this community for twenty years. Every cobweb cupcake, every spider leg soufflé – it's all been for Hollow Creek. I love this town, quirks and all."

Morty's voice softened, but his intensity remained. "And that's why I can't let this go. Someone's trying to frame me, sure. But more importantly, there's a killer out there. And I won't rest until they're caught – no matter who they turn out to be."

Mayor Candy Corn's face reddened, his jowls quivering with rage. "You're making a grave mistake, Graves!"

Morty couldn't help but chuckle. "Was that pun intentional, Mr. Mayor? Because I have to say, it's not your best work."

The mayor slammed his fist on the desk, rattling a bowl of candy corn. "This isn't a joke! You're threatening the very fabric of our community!"

Morty's eyes narrowed. He leaned in close, his voice dropping to a whisper. "No, Cornelius. You are. With your cover-ups and your backroom deals. I know about the missing funds from last year's festival. I know about the zoning 'irregularities' with that new development."

Mayor Candy Corn's smirk faltered. Sweat beaded on his brow.

Morty pressed on, fueled by the support of his friends and the townspeople who believed in him. "Here's how this is going to go. You're going to step aside. Let the investigation proceed without interference. Or I'll make sure every skeleton in your closet comes dancing out for all to see."

The mayor's eyes darted around the room, as if seeking an escape. But Morty stood firm, his wild hair seeming to crackle with determination.

"You wouldn't dare," the mayor hissed.

Morty grinned, a glint in his eye. "Try me. I've got a recipe for disaster with your name on it, Candy Corn."

Mayor Candy Corn's face contorted, cycling through shades of red and purple. He tugged at his candy corn-patterned tie, loosening it as if it were choking him. Finally, he slumped back in his chair, deflated.

"Fine," he spat. "The investigation can continue. But mark my words, Graves. If you fail to find the real killer, you'll wish you'd never set foot in my office."

Morty straightened up, adjusting his apron adorned with dancing skeletons. "Is that a threat, Mr. Mayor?"

"It's a promise," Candy Corn sneered. "You're cooking up trouble, and if it boils over, you'll be the one getting burned."

Morty couldn't resist one last jab. "Well, I've always liked my justice served hot. Now, if you'll excuse me, I have a killer to catch and a reputation to clear."

He turned on his heel, his resolve as firm as a well-baked cookie. As he reached for the doorknob, the mayor's voice stopped him.

"Remember, Graves. The clock is ticking. Tick-tock, tick-tock."

Morty paused, his hand on the door. Without turning back, he replied, "Good thing I'm used to working under pressure. It's how I make my ghost pepper soufflé rise."

Morty stepped out of the mayor's office, the door clicking shut behind him. The hallway seemed to stretch endlessly, its walls adorned with portraits of past mayors. Their painted eyes seemed to follow him, judging.

He took a deep breath, the scent of lemon-scented cleaner mingling with the faint aroma of candy corn that clung to everything in this building. His mind raced, processing the confrontation.

"Well, that went about as smoothly as my first attempt at blood pudding," Morty muttered to himself, chuckling darkly.

He made his way down the stairs, each step echoing in the empty stairwell. The weight of the encounter pressed down on him, heavier than his prized cast-iron cauldron.

Outside, the crisp autumn air hit him like a slap to the face. Morty paused on the steps of Town Hall, watching fallen leaves dance across the sidewalk. The setting sun cast long shadows, turning Hollow Creek into a tableau of orange and black.

"This isn't over," he thought, clenching his fists. "Not by a long shot."

A chill ran down his spine, and not just from the evening breeze. He knew Mayor Candy Corn wouldn't give up easily. The battle lines were drawn, and Morty was ready for war.

As he started walking home, a sudden rustling in the nearby bushes made him freeze. A pair of glowing eyes stared back at him from the darkness.

"Who's there?" Morty called out, his heart pounding. "Show yourself, or I'll-"

CHAPTER 5

The bell above the door of Willow's Whispers jangled violently as Morty Graves burst in, his chef's hat askew and his eyes wild. Crystals clinked and candles flickered in his wake. Willow Shadowmoon looked up from her tarot cards, her violet eyes widening.

"Willow! I need your help!" Morty panted, his portly frame heaving. "It's a matter of life and death!"

Willow rose gracefully, her shimmering robes swirling. "Calm yourself, Mortimer. The spirits cannot speak through such chaos."

Morty's hands flailed. "But Ima Picky is dead! Murdered! And they think I did it!"

Willow's eyebrow arched. She studied Morty's desperate face. Could this jovial chef truly be a killer? She sensed no malice, only panic and... was that tomato sauce on his apron?

"What exactly do you require of me?" Willow asked cautiously.

"Your psychic powers!" Morty exclaimed. "You can prove my innocence!"

Willow hesitated. Murder investigations were dangerous territory. She valued her reputation in Hollow Creek. But the genuine fear in Morty's eyes tugged at her.

"This is no simple tarot reading, Mortimer," she warned. "The consequences could be grave."

Morty's mustache twitched. "Graver than being accused of murder? Ha! Now that's a grave situation!"

Willow sighed. Even facing prison, Morty couldn't resist a pun. She weighed her options carefully. The risks were high, but so was the potential to prove her abilities once and for all.

"Very well," she said finally. "But I must warn you—"

A crash from the back room cut her off. Both Morty and Willow whirled to face the sound, hearts racing. What new danger lurked in the shadows?

Willow held up a hand, silencing Morty's impending outburst. She glided toward the beaded curtain separating her shop from the storage area.

"It's likely just my familiar," she whispered, though doubt tinged her voice.

Morty's eyes widened. "You have a familiar? Is it a black cat? A raven? A ghostly apparition?"

Willow shot him an exasperated look. "It's a hamster named Mr. Whiskers."

Despite the tension, Morty snorted. Willow ignored him, focusing her energy on the room beyond. She sensed no malevolent presence, just a faint aura of... mischief?

Cautiously, she parted the curtain. A small, furry blur zoomed past her feet, followed by a cascade of tumbling tarot cards.

"Mr. Whiskers!" Willow scolded, her mystical demeanor momentarily forgotten. "Those are antique!"

Morty chuckled, tension easing from his shoulders. "Some familiar. Can he predict my future? Or just the weather in his exercise wheel?"

Willow straightened, smoothing her robes. "Mock not the vessels through which the universe speaks, Mortimer."

She turned to face him, violet eyes intense. "Now, about your request. I will assist you, but you must understand the limitations of my gift."

Morty nodded eagerly. "Anything, Willow. You're my only hope!"

"My visions are not always clear," she explained. "I can gather impressions, glimpses of truth, but interpreting them is..."

A loud squeak interrupted her. Mr. Whiskers had returned, proudly dragging the Death card in his tiny paws.

Morty paled. "Is... is that a sign?"

Willow sighed. This case was going to be more challenging than she'd anticipated.

Willow waved her hand dismissively at the hamster's antics. "Let's focus, shall we?"

She led Morty to a round table draped in deep purple velvet. Crystal balls and scattered runes adorned its surface. Morty eyed them warily as he sat.

"Now," Willow began, "tell me everything you know about our suspects."

Morty's brow furrowed. "Well, there's Bella Notte, my sous chef. Ambitious, but loyal. Mayor Candy Corn, always scheming. And... well, you."

Willow raised an eyebrow. "Me?"

"Hey, I'm just covering all bases," Morty shrugged, his chef's hat wobbling precariously.

Willow pursed her lips. "Very well. Let's begin."

She closed her eyes, breathing deeply. The shop's incense grew thicker, swirling around them. Morty watched, fascinated, as Willow's face relaxed into a trance-like state.

"I see... shadows," she murmured. "Flashes of... kitchen knives? A broken pumpkin. Anger, fear, ambition..."

Morty leaned forward, nearly knocking over a candle. "What does it mean?"

Willow's eyes snapped open. "It means, Mortimer, that this case is far more complex than we imagined."

Suddenly, the shop's door burst open. A figure stood silhouetted in the doorway, brandishing what looked suspiciously like a wooden spoon.

"Morty Graves!" a shrill voice cried. "I know you're in here!"

Morty ducked under the table, hissing, "It's Ima Picky! Quick, tell her I've been abducted by spirits!"

Willow rolled her eyes at Morty's theatrics. She raised her voice, addressing the intruder. "Madame Picky, this is a private consultation. Please return later."

The door slammed shut. Willow sighed, refocusing on the task at hand. "Now, about Bella Notte..."

She closed her eyes again, her fingers tracing patterns in the air. "I see... a young woman, wide-eyed, clutching a chef's knife. She's scared, but determined."

Morty peeked out from under the table. "That's Bella, alright. Always nervous, that one."

Willow nodded, her brow furrowing. "There's more. I sense... admiration. No, devotion. She sees you as a mentor, Morty. But also..."

"Also what?" Morty prompted, fully emerging now.

"A barrier," Willow finished. "She dreams of her own kitchen, her own acclaim. But your shadow looms large."

Morty's mustache drooped. "Bella? But she's like a daughter to me!"

Willow opened her eyes, her gaze piercing. "Sometimes, Mortimer, that's precisely the problem."

She paused, letting the revelation sink in. Then, with a flourish of her robes, she continued. "Now, for our esteemed mayor..."

As she delved into her next vision, the shop's lights flickered ominously. Morty glanced around nervously, wondering what other surprises this investigation might reveal.

Willow's eyes snapped open, her violet irises glowing with an otherworldly intensity. "Morty, I... I need to confess something."

Morty leaned forward, his wild hair crackling with static. "What is it, Willow? Did you see something about the mayor?"

She shook her head, crystals tinkling softly around her neck. "No, it's about me. About Ima Picky."

Morty's bushy eyebrows shot up. "You? But you're not a suspect!"

Willow sighed, her slender fingers tracing the edge of her crystal ball. "When Ima publicly doubted my abilities, I felt... angry. Furious, even."

"Well, that's understandable," Morty chuckled nervously. "Ima's tongue is sharper than my best filleting knife."

"You don't understand," Willow whispered. "For a moment, I wanted to... to silence her."

Morty's face paled beneath his chef's hat. "You mean...?"

Willow's eyes widened. "No! Not murder. Never that. But I wanted to prove her wrong, to make her eat her words."

Morty relaxed visibly. "Oh, is that all? I think we've all felt that way about Ima at some point."

Willow nodded solemnly. "Still, I needed you to know. Now, let me continue my psychic probing."

She closed her eyes again, her brow furrowing in concentration. Suddenly, she gasped.

"What? What is it?" Morty asked, nearly knocking over a jar of eye of newt in his excitement.

"I see... a red feather. And... the smell of cinnamon. There's a connection here, Morty. Something important."

Morty's eyes lit up, a grin spreading across his face. "A red feather? Cinnamon? By the great pumpkin, Willow, you're onto something!"

He leapt from his chair, pacing the cramped shop. His apron, adorned with tiny skulls, fluttered with each step.

"Mayor Candy Corn," Morty mused, tapping his chin. "He always wears that ridiculous red feather in his hat. And Bella Notte... her signature dish is cinnamon-spiced pumpkin soup!"

Willow's eyes snapped open. "You're right. But how are they connected?"

Morty stopped pacing, his face grave. "What if... what if this isn't just about me? What if someone's trying to ruin Halloween itself?"

Willow gasped, her hand flying to her mouth. "The festival! It's the town's biggest event. If it fails..."

"Hollow Creek would never be the same," Morty finished grimly.

A chill ran through the room, making the candles flicker. Willow shivered, pulling her flowing robes tighter.

"Morty," she said softly, "I fear we're treading into dangerous waters. This is bigger than we imagined."

Morty nodded, his usual jovial demeanor replaced by determination. "What do you suggest?"

Willow's eyes gleamed with sudden inspiration. "Dr. Frankie Stein. She has connections, resources. We need her help."

Morty's face lit up. "Brilliant! Dr. Stein's the perfect person to help us unravel this mystery."

He reached for his phone, pausing before dialing. "Willow, I can't thank you enough. Your insights are invaluable."

Willow smiled, a rare occurrence that softened her usually intense features. "Just promise to keep me in the loop, Morty. I'm invested now."

"You have my word," Morty replied, his tone solemn despite the pumpkin-shaped charm dangling from his phone case.

As they prepared to leave, Willow's shop seemed to whisper around them. Crystals glinted, tarot cards rustled.

Morty felt a pang of reluctance. The cozy, incense-scented space had become a sanctuary of sorts.

At the door, he turned to Willow. "Stay safe, okay? We don't know who we're dealing with."

Willow nodded, her violet eyes fierce. "You too, Morty. The spirits are restless. Be cautious."

They stepped out into the chilly evening. Jack-o'-lanterns grinned from nearby porches, their eerie light a reminder of what was at stake.

"I'll head to Dr. Stein's lab," Morty said. "You?"

"Back to my crystals," Willow replied. "There's more to uncover."

As they parted ways, a black cat darted across their path. Morty couldn't shake the feeling that their real adventure was just beginning.

Morty watched Willow's retreating form, her robes swishing mysteriously in the twilight. He turned towards Dr. Stein's lab, his mind racing.

"What a pickle I'm in," he muttered. "Or should I say, what a pumpkin?"

He chuckled at his own joke, then sobered. The weight of the situation pressed down on him like an oversized chef's hat.

As he walked, shadows danced at the edge of his vision. Was someone following him? He quickened his pace, his heartbeat a frantic drumroll.

"Get it together, Morty," he whispered. "You're just being paranoid. Like that time you thought the gingerbread men were plotting against you."

But the feeling persisted. He glanced back, seeing nothing but jack-o'-lanterns leering from every porch.

Suddenly, a figure loomed before him. Morty yelped, stumbling backward.

"Watch where you're going, you overgrown pumpkin!" a familiar voice snapped.

Morty blinked. It was just Mayor Candy Corn, looking irritated.

"S-sorry, Mayor," Morty stammered. "I'm a bit on edge."

The Mayor's eyes narrowed. "Aren't we all? With a murderer on the loose..."

As Candy Corn walked away, Morty couldn't shake a chill that had nothing to do with the autumn air.

He hurried on, Dr. Stein's lab now in sight. But as he reached for the door, a blood-curdling scream split the night.

CHAPTER 6

The bell above the door of Willow's Whispers jangled violently as Morty Graves burst in, his chef's hat askew and his eyes wild. Crystals clinked and candles flickered in his wake. Willow Shadowmoon looked up from her tarot cards, her violet eyes widening.

"Willow! I need your help!" Morty panted, his frame heaving. "It's a matter of life and death!"

Willow rose gracefully, her shimmering robes swirling. "Calm yourself, Mortimer. The spirits cannot speak through such chaos."

Morty's hands flailed. "But Ima Picky is dead! Murdered! And they think I did it!"

Willow's eyebrow arched. She studied Morty's desperate face. Could this jovial chef truly be a killer? She sensed no malice, only panic and... was that tomato sauce on his apron?

"What exactly do you require of me?" Willow asked cautiously.

"Your psychic powers!" Morty exclaimed. "You can prove my innocence!"

Willow hesitated. Murder investigations were dangerous territory. She valued her reputation in Hollow Creek. But the genuine fear in Morty's eyes tugged at her.

"This is no simple tarot reading, Mortimer," she warned. "The consequences could be grave."

Morty's mustache twitched. "Graver than being accused of murder? Ha! Now that's a grave situation!"

Willow sighed. Even facing prison, Morty couldn't resist a pun. She weighed her options carefully. The risks were high, but so was the potential to prove her abilities once and for all.

"Very well," she said finally. "But I must warn you—"

A crash from the back room cut her off. Both Morty and Willow whirled to face the sound, hearts racing. What new danger lurked in the shadows?

Willow held up a hand, silencing Morty's impending outburst. She glided toward the beaded curtain separating her shop from the storage area.

"It's likely just my familiar," she whispered, though doubt tinged her voice.

Morty's eyes widened. "You have a familiar? Is it a black cat? A raven? A ghostly apparition?"

Willow shot him an exasperated look. "It's a hamster named Mr. Whiskers."

Despite the tension, Morty snorted. Willow ignored him, focusing her energy on the room beyond. She sensed no malevolent presence, just a faint aura of... mischief?

Cautiously, she parted the curtain. A small, furry blur zoomed past her feet, followed by a cascade of tumbling tarot cards.

"Mr. Whiskers!" Willow scolded, her mystical demeanor momentarily forgotten. "Those are antique!"

Morty chuckled, tension easing from his shoulders. "Some familiar. Can he predict my future? Or just the weather in his exercise wheel?"

Willow straightened, smoothing her robes. "Mock not the vessels through which the universe speaks, Mortimer."

She turned to face him, violet eyes intense. "Now, about your request. I will assist you, but you must understand the limitations of my gift."

Morty nodded eagerly. "Anything, Willow. You're my only hope!"

"My visions are not always clear," she explained. "I can gather impressions, glimpses of truth, but interpreting them is..."

A loud squeak interrupted her. Mr. Whiskers had returned, proudly dragging the Death card in his tiny paws.

Morty paled. "Is... is that a sign?"

Willow sighed. This case was going to be more challenging than she'd anticipated.

Willow waved her hand dismissively at the hamster's antics. "Let's focus, shall we?"

She led Morty to a round table draped in deep purple velvet. Crystal balls and scattered runes adorned its surface. Morty eyed them warily as he sat.

"Now," Willow began, "tell me everything you know about our suspects."

Morty's brow furrowed. "Well, there's Bella Notte, my sous chef. Ambitious, but loyal. Mayor Candy Corn, always scheming. And... well, you."

Willow raised an eyebrow. "Me?"

"Hey, I'm just covering all bases," Morty shrugged, his chef's hat wobbling precariously.

Willow pursed her lips. "Very well. Let's begin."

She closed her eyes, breathing deeply. The shop's incense grew thicker, swirling around them. Morty watched, fascinated, as Willow's face relaxed into a trance-like state.

"I see... shadows," she murmured. "Flashes of... kitchen knives? A broken pumpkin. Anger, fear, ambition..."

Morty leaned forward, nearly knocking over a candle. "What does it mean?"

Willow's eyes snapped open. "It means, Mortimer, that this case is far more complex than we imagined."

Suddenly, the shop's door burst open. A figure stood silhouetted in the doorway, brandishing what looked suspiciously like a wooden spoon.

"Morty Graves!" a shrill voice cried. "I know you're in here!"

Morty ducked under the table, hissing, "It's Ima Picky! Quick, tell her I've been abducted by spirits!"

Willow rolled her eyes at Morty's theatrics. She raised her voice, addressing the intruder. "Madame Picky, this is a private consultation. Please return later."

The door slammed shut. Willow sighed, refocusing on the task at hand. "Now, about Bella Notte..."

She closed her eyes again, her fingers tracing patterns in the air. "I see... a young woman, wide-eyed, clutching a chef's knife. She's scared, but determined."

Morty peeked out from under the table. "That's Bella, alright. Always nervous, that one."

Willow nodded, her brow furrowing. "There's more. I sense... admiration. No, devotion. She sees you as a mentor, Morty. But also..."

"Also what?" Morty prompted, fully emerging now.

"A barrier," Willow finished. "She dreams of her own kitchen, her own acclaim. But your shadow looms large."

Morty's mustache drooped. "Bella? But she's like a daughter to me!"

Willow opened her eyes, her gaze piercing. "Sometimes, Mortimer, that's precisely the problem."

She paused, letting the revelation sink in. Then, with a flourish of her robes, she continued. "Now, for our esteemed mayor..."

As she delved into her next vision, the shop's lights flickered ominously. Morty glanced around nervously, wondering what other surprises this investigation might reveal.

Willow's eyes snapped open, her violet irises glowing with an otherworldly intensity. "Morty, I... I need to confess something."

Morty leaned forward, his wild hair crackling with static. "What is it, Willow? Did you see something about the mayor?"

She shook her head, crystals tinkling softly around her neck. "No, it's about me. About Ima Picky."

Morty's bushy eyebrows shot up. "You? But you're not a suspect!"

Willow sighed, her slender fingers tracing the edge of her crystal ball. "When Ima publicly doubted my abilities, I felt... angry. Furious, even."

"Well, that's understandable," Morty chuckled nervously. "Ima's tongue is sharper than my best filleting knife."

"You don't understand," Willow whispered. "For a moment, I wanted to... to silence her."

Morty's face paled beneath his chef's hat. "You mean...?"

Willow's eyes widened. "No! Not murder. Never that. But I wanted to prove her wrong, to make her eat her words."

Morty relaxed visibly. "Oh, is that all? I think we've all felt that way about Ima at some point."

Willow nodded solemnly. "Still, I needed you to know. Now, let me continue my psychic probing."

She closed her eyes again, her brow furrowing in concentration. Suddenly, she gasped.

"What? What is it?" Morty asked, nearly knocking over a jar of eye of newt in his excitement.

"I see... a red feather. And... the smell of cinnamon. There's a connection here, Morty. Something important."

Morty's eyes lit up, a grin spreading across his face. "A red feather? Cinnamon? By the great pumpkin, Willow, you're onto something!"

He leapt from his chair, pacing the cramped shop. His apron, adorned with tiny skulls, fluttered with each step.

"Mayor Candy Corn," Morty mused, tapping his chin. "He always wears that ridiculous red feather in his hat. And Bella Notte... her signature dish is cinnamon-spiced pumpkin soup!"

Willow's violet eyes snapped open. "You're right. But how are they connected?"

Morty stopped pacing, his face grave. "What if... what if this isn't just about me? What if someone's trying to ruin Halloween itself?"

Willow gasped, her hand flying to her mouth. "The festival! It's the town's biggest event. If it fails..."

"Hollow Creek would never be the same," Morty finished grimly.

A chill ran through the room, making the candles flicker. Willow shivered, pulling her flowing robes tighter.

"Morty," she said softly, "I fear we're treading into dangerous waters. This is bigger than we imagined."

Morty nodded, his usual jovial demeanor replaced by determination. "What do you suggest?"

Willow's eyes gleamed with sudden inspiration. "Dr. Frankie Stein. She has connections, resources. We need her help."

Morty's face lit up. "Brilliant! Dr. Stein's the perfect person to help us unravel this mystery."

He reached for his phone, pausing before dialing. "Willow, I can't thank you enough. Your insights are invaluable."

Willow smiled, a rare occurrence that softened her usually intense features. "Just promise to keep me in the loop, Morty. I'm invested now."

"You have my word," Morty replied, his tone solemn despite the pumpkin-shaped charm dangling from his phone case.

As they prepared to leave, Willow's shop seemed to whisper around them. Crystals glinted, tarot cards rustled.

Morty felt a pang of reluctance. The cozy, incense-scented space had become a sanctuary of sorts.

At the door, he turned to Willow. "Stay safe, okay? We don't know who we're dealing with."

Willow nodded, her violet eyes fierce. "You too, Morty. The spirits are restless. Be cautious."

They stepped out into the chilly evening. Jack-o'-lanterns grinned from nearby porches, their eerie light a reminder of what was at stake.

"I'll head to Dr. Stein's lab," Morty said. "You?"

"Back to my crystals," Willow replied. "There's more to uncover."

As they parted ways, a black cat darted across their path. Morty couldn't shake the feeling that their real adventure was just beginning.

Morty watched Willow's retreating form, her robes swishing mysteriously in the twilight. He turned towards Dr. Stein's lab, his mind racing.

"What a pickle I'm in," he muttered. "Or should I say, what a pumpkin?"

He chuckled at his own joke, then sobered. The weight of the situation pressed down on him like an oversized chef's hat.

As he walked, shadows danced at the edge of his vision. Was someone following him? He quickened his pace, his heartbeat a frantic drumroll.

"Get it together, Morty," he whispered. "You're just being paranoid. Like that time you thought the gingerbread men were plotting against you."

But the feeling persisted. He glanced back, seeing nothing but jack-o'-lanterns leering from every porch.

Suddenly, a figure loomed before him. Morty yelped, stumbling backward.

"Watch where you're going, you overgrown pumpkin!" a familiar voice snapped.

Morty blinked. It was just Mayor Candy Corn, looking irritated.

"S-sorry, Mayor," Morty stammered. "I'm a bit on edge."

The Mayor's eyes narrowed. "Aren't we all? With a murderer on the loose..."

As Candy Corn walked away, Morty couldn't shake a chill that had nothing to do with the autumn air.

Patti Petrone Miller

He hurried on, Dr. Stein's lab now in sight. But as he reached for the door, a blood-curdling scream split the night.

CHAPTER 7

The Ghoulish Gourmet's office smelled of pumpkin spice and formaldehyde. Morty shuffled papers on his cluttered desk, searching for the coroner's report. Willow perched on a nearby chair, her violet eyes scanning the room.

"What do you make of the claw marks on the victim?" Morty asked, frowning at a photo.

Willow leaned closer. "They seem... unnatural. Almost ritualistic."

Her flowery perfume mingled with the office's odd scents. Morty's heart quickened. He tried to focus on the evidence, not her proximity.

"Could be from some kind of occult ceremony," he mused. "Or just a very angry cat."

Willow's lips twitched. "Your humor is as dark as your recipes, Mortimer."

"Please, call me Morty. All my friends do." He paused. "Well, both of them."

She laughed, a sound like wind chimes. "You have more friends than you realize."

Morty's cheeks warmed. He reached for another file, his hand accidentally brushing Willow's. A literal spark crackled between them. They both jerked back.

"Static electricity," Morty muttered. But the tingling in his fingers felt different. Stronger.

Willow's eyes widened. "Did you feel that?"

"The spark? Yeah, must be the carpet—"

"No," she interrupted. "The energy. It was... powerful."

Morty's mind raced. What did she mean? He'd felt something, sure, but...

"Let's, uh, get back to the case," he said quickly. "What about the weird symbols found near the body?"

Willow nodded, but her gaze lingered on him. "Of course. Those markings could be significant..."

As they dove back into theories, Morty couldn't shake the lingering sensation from their touch. Something had changed, subtle but undeniable. He just wasn't sure what.

Morty's heart pounded as he stared at the evidence spread before them. But his mind was elsewhere. The spark, Willow's intense gaze, the strange energy between them... it all swirled in his thoughts.

He cleared his throat. "Willow, I... I need to tell you something."

She looked up, "What is it, Morty?"

He took a deep breath. "I've never met anyone quite like you before. Someone who truly understands my passion for the macabre, for the mysteries that lurk in the shadows."

Willow's eyebrows rose. Morty plunged on, his words tumbling out.

"You don't just tolerate my obsession with spooky cuisine, you embrace it. You see the beauty in the darkness, just like I do. And I... I find myself drawn to that. To you."

He exhaled, feeling both terrified and relieved. Willow sat perfectly still, her expression unreadable.

"Oh no," Morty thought. "I've completely misread this. She probably thinks I'm a lunatic now."

But then Willow's face softened. "Morty," she said gently. "I... I'm not sure what to say. I'm taken aback, truly."

Morty's heart sank. "I understand. I shouldn't have-"

"No," Willow interrupted. "Let me finish. I'm surprised because... well, I feel the same way."

Now it was Morty's turn to be shocked. "You do?"

Willow nodded, a faint blush coloring her cheeks. "Your creativity, your warmth... it's captivating. I've always been drawn to it, to you. Your ability to find joy in the macabre, to create beauty from the bizarre... it's remarkable."

Morty felt lightheaded. Was this really happening?

"I've never met anyone who sees the world quite the way you do," Willow continued. "It's... refreshing. Exhilarating, even."

They stared at each other, the air between them charged with unspoken emotions. The murder investigation lay forgotten on the desk, overshadowed by this unexpected revelation.

Morty's heart raced. He leaned in, drawn by an invisible force. Willow mirrored his movement. Their faces were inches apart now. He could smell her lavender perfume, feel her warm breath.

"Willow," he whispered, his voice husky. "May I-"

She answered by closing the gap. Their lips met, tentative at first, then with growing passion. Morty's mind exploded with sensations. The softness of her lips. The taste of peppermint. The warmth of her hand on his cheek.

Time seemed to stand still. When they finally parted, both were breathless.

"Well," Morty chuckled nervously. "That was... spellbinding."

Willow laughed, her eyes sparkling. "Trust you to find a spooky way to describe a kiss."

Morty grinned, feeling giddy. His mind whirled with possibilities. He didn't want this moment to end.

"Willow," he said suddenly. "What do you say we take a break from all this grim detective work?"

She raised an eyebrow. "What did you have in mind?"

"A date," Morty replied, surprising himself with his boldness. "Let's celebrate this... connection. We could grab dinner, or maybe-"

"Yes," Willow interrupted, beaming. "I'd love that."

Morty's heart soared. He stood, offering his hand. "Shall we, then? I know just the place."

As they left the office, Morty's mind raced with ideas. He'd make this a night to remember, filled with all the eerie delights they both adored.

Willow's eyes widened as they approached the dilapidated Victorian mansion. Neon signs flickered, spelling out "Hollow Creek's Haunted Haven" in sickly green letters.

"Oh, Morty," she breathed. "It's perfect."

Morty grinned, pleased with his choice. "I thought you'd appreciate a bit of supernatural ambiance for our first date."

They approached the ticket booth, manned by a bored-looking teenager in zombie makeup. Morty fumbled for his wallet, but Willow beat him to it.

"My treat," she said with a wink. "Consider it a thank you for that delightful kiss earlier."

Morty felt his cheeks flush. "Well, I certainly can't argue with that logic."

As they entered the attraction, spooky music filled the air. Fog machines created an eerie atmosphere, and fake cobwebs clung to every surface.

Willow slipped her hand into Morty's, intertwining their fingers. The simple gesture sent a jolt through him, more thrilling than any haunted house scare.

"Ready to face some ghosts?" he asked, giving her hand a gentle squeeze.

Willow's eyes sparkled mischievously. "Darling, I commune with spirits daily. This should be a walk in the park."

They stepped into the first room, dimly lit by flickering candles. Suddenly, a mechanical ghost popped out from behind a curtain, wailing dramatically.

Morty jumped, embarrassingly high. Willow, true to her word, didn't flinch.

"My," she said dryly, "how terrifying."

Morty chuckled, his heart racing more from her proximity than the scare. "Well, not all of us have your supernatural prowess, my dear."

As they moved through the attraction, Morty found himself paying more attention to Willow than the scares. The way her eyes lit up at each new room. The soft pressure of her hand in his. The musical sound of her laughter.

"You know," he said as they entered a room designed to look like a mad scientist's lab, "I'm beginning to think this was the best idea I've ever had."

A mechanical arm swung down from the ceiling, clutching a pulsating, rubber "brain." Willow ducked, pulling Morty with her.

"Nice reflexes," Morty grinned, his face inches from hers.

Willow smirked. "Years of dodging my grandmother's attempts to set me up with 'nice young men.'"

They straightened up, still holding hands. Morty's thumb traced small circles on her palm.

"Speaking of family," he began, his voice softening, "I've been meaning to tell you about mine."

Willow tilted her head, curiosity evident in her eyes. "Oh?"

Before Morty could continue, a person in a werewolf costume leaped out from behind a curtain, howling loudly.

Morty yelped, then laughed at himself. "Curse these jump scares! They get me every time."

Willow chuckled, squeezing his hand reassuringly. "It's endearing. Now, what were you saying about your family?"

Morty took a deep breath. The haunted house suddenly felt very small, very intimate.

"Well, you see, the Graves family has always been... different. Our culinary traditions aren't exactly normal."

They moved into the next room, decorated like a Victorian séance parlor. Fake candles flickered on a round table.

"Different how?" Willow prompted gently.

Morty's eyes darted around, making sure no other guests were within earshot. "We've always cooked with a touch of the supernatural. Family legend says my great-great-grandmother could summon spirits with her beef stew."

Willow's violet eyes widened. "That's... incredible."

Morty nodded, a mix of pride and uncertainty in his expression. "It's why I opened The Ghoulish Gourmet. To honor that legacy."

They paused in front of a creaky old mirror. Their reflections wavered, distorted.

"But sometimes," Morty continued, his voice barely above a whisper, "I wonder if I'm doing enough. If I'm living up to their expectations."

Willow turned to face him, her gaze intense. "Morty, your talent is undeniable. The way you blend the macabre with culinary artistry... it's pure magic."

A ghostly apparition floated through the room, but neither of them noticed.

"You really think so?" Morty asked, his usual bravado momentarily absent.

Willow nodded emphatically. "I've seen how your food brings joy, even in its spookiest forms. That's a rare gift."

Morty's chest swelled with emotion. He opened his mouth to respond, but was interrupted by a mechanical skeleton dropping from the ceiling.

They both jumped, then burst into laughter.

"Maybe we should continue this conversation somewhere less... jumpy," Morty suggested.

Willow grinned. "Lead the way, Chef Graves."

They exited the haunted house, the cool night air a stark contrast to the stuffy interior.

"How about dinner at The Ghoulish Gourmet?" Morty proposed. "I have an idea for a special dish."

Willow's eyes sparkled with intrigue. "I wouldn't miss it for the world."

The Ghoulish Gourmet's kitchen hummed with energy as Morty bustled about, his hands a flurry of motion. Willow perched on a stool, watching him work with rapt attention.

"So," Morty said, deftly chopping a blood-red beet, "about Ima's murder. What's our next move?"

Willow drummed her fingers on the countertop. "We need to revisit the crime scene. I sense there's something we missed."

Morty nodded, sliding the beets into a bubbling cauldron. "Agreed. But we'll need a distraction for Sheriff Bonecrusher."

"Leave that to me," Willow said, a mischievous glint in her eye. "I'll conjure up a spectral diversion."

Morty raised an eyebrow. "You can do that?"

Willow winked. "A psychic never reveals her secrets."

They shared a laugh, the tension of the investigation momentarily forgotten.

"What about suspects?" Morty mused, stirring the cauldron. "That rival food critic, Boris Biteworthy, seemed awfully eager to take Ima's place."

Willow's brow furrowed. "True. And don't forget Ima's assistant, Penelope Parchment. She inherited quite a bit from Ima's will."

The kitchen fell silent save for the bubbling of the cauldron. Morty's mind raced with possibilities.

"We're missing something," he muttered. "A crucial ingredient in this mystery stew."

Willow reached across the counter, her hand brushing Morty's. "We'll figure it out together."

Morty's heart skipped a beat. He cleared his throat. "Right. Together."

He ladled the steaming concoction into two skull-shaped bowls. "Dinner is served. I call it 'Bloody Secrets Soup.'"

Willow's eyes widened as she took a spoonful. "It's... hauntingly delicious."

As they ate, they continued to dissect the case, their theories growing wilder with each bite. The night deepened around them, full of promise and peril.

Morty walked Willow to her front porch, their footsteps crunching on the gravel driveway. The moon hung low, casting long shadows across the lawn. Crickets chirped in the distance.

"Well," Morty said, his voice husky. "This is you."

Willow turned, her eyes sparkling in the moonlight. "So it is."

They stood in silence, neither wanting the night to end. Morty's heart raced. He fumbled for words.

"I, uh... I had a wonderful time tonight," he managed.

Willow smiled. "Me too. Who knew discussing murder could be so... romantic?"

Morty chuckled. "Only us, I suppose."

Their laughter faded, replaced by a charged silence. Morty leaned in, drawn by an invisible force. Willow met him halfway.

Their lips touched, soft and tentative at first, then with growing passion. Morty's world narrowed to the sensation of Willow in his arms, the scent of her perfume, the taste of her lips.

When they finally parted, both were breathless.

"Wow," Willow whispered.

"Yeah," Morty agreed, dazed. "Wow indeed."

They gazed at each other, grinning like lovestruck teenagers.

"So," Willow said, "same time tomorrow? For the investigation, I mean."

Morty nodded eagerly. "Absolutely. We'll crack this case yet."

"And maybe..." Willow trailed off, blushing.

"Maybe explore this... us... a bit more?" Morty finished.

Willow nodded, her smile radiant.

As Morty turned to leave, a twig snapped in the darkness. Both froze.

"Did you hear that?" Willow whispered.
Morty's eyes scanned the shadows. "Someone's watching us."

CHAPTER 6

Morty's fingers twitched as he approached Dr. Frankie Stein's lair. The dilapidated Victorian mansion loomed before him, its windows like hollow eyes. He steeled himself and rapped on the door.

A moment later, it creaked open. Dr. Frankie stood there, silhouetted against flickering candlelight.

"Ah, Mortimer. To what do I owe this... unexpected pleasure?" Her voice was cool, unruffled.

Morty's eyes narrowed. "Cut the pleasantries, Doc. I know you were connected to Ima Picky. I want answers. Now."

Dr. Frankie raised an eyebrow. "My, how direct. Please, do come in."

She led him to a cluttered study. Beakers bubbled ominously. A raven cawed from its perch.

Morty planted himself in front of her desk. "Spill it, Frankie. What's your involvement in Ima's murder?"

Dr. Frankie steepled her fingers. "I assure you, Mortimer, I am not the killer."

"But you knew her."

"Indeed. We had a... rather unpleasant encounter in the past."

Morty's pulse quickened. "Go on."

"It was years ago. But I've been working tirelessly to uncover the truth behind her demise."

Morty scoffed. "And why should I believe you?"

Dr. Frankie's green eyes flashed. "Because, my dear Mortimer, I may be your only ally in this tangled web of deceit."

Morty's mind raced. Could he trust her? Or was she playing him like one of her arcane experiments?

He needed more. But for now, he'd hear her out. The truth was out there, hidden in the shadows of Hollow Creek. And he'd be damned if he didn't uncover it.

Morty's fingers drummed against his thigh. Trust didn't come easy, especially not in Hollow Creek during these dark times. But Dr. Frankie Stein was offering answers. He'd be a fool not to listen.

"Alright, Doc," he said, settling into a creaky armchair. "Let's hear it. What's this unpleasant encounter you mentioned?"

Dr. Frankie's lips curled into a wry smile. "It was at the Annual Culinary Confluence of Cryptids and Creatures. Five years ago, to be precise."

Morty's eyebrows shot up. "The ACCCC? That's not an easy ticket to snag."

"Indeed. I was there presenting my latest creation - a sentient soufflé."

"Sounds... interesting," Morty offered, trying not to imagine the implications.

Dr. Frankie waved a hand dismissively. "It was revolutionary. But Ima... she had other thoughts."

The doctor's eyes grew distant, reliving the memory. Morty leaned forward, hanging on every word.

"I was mid-presentation when Ima burst in," Dr. Frankie continued. "She declared my soufflé an abomination. Said I was mocking the culinary arts."

Morty winced. He could picture Ima's cutting remarks, sharp as a chef's knife.

"She didn't stop there," Dr. Frankie said, her voice dropping to a near-whisper. "She rallied the crowd. They jeered. They laughed. My poor soufflé... it became self-aware just in time to realize it was being mocked. It deflated on the spot."

"Ouch," Morty muttered. He'd faced Ima's wrath before, but this sounded particularly brutal.

Dr. Frankie's eyes refocused, locking onto Morty's. "It was humiliating, yes. But I assure you, Mortimer, I did not kill Ima Picky over a dessert gone wrong."

Morty studied her face, searching for any hint of deception. "That's quite a story, Doc. But why keep it secret until now?"

"Would you proudly advertise such a public failure?" Dr. Frankie countered.

He had to admit, she had a point. Still, something nagged at him. "So if you're not the killer, why get involved at all?"

Dr. Frankie leaned back, a mysterious smile playing on her lips. "Let's just say I have a vested interest in uncovering the truth. Hollow Creek holds many secrets, Mortimer. Ima's death is merely the tip of the iceberg."

Morty felt a chill run down his spine. What exactly had he stumbled into?

Morty leaned forward, his brow furrowed. "Alright, Doc. You've got my attention. But motive isn't everything. Where were you when Ima met her untimely demise?"

Dr. Frankie's smile widened. She reached into her flowing black coat and produced a sleek tablet. "I thought you might ask that," she said, tapping the screen with long, pale fingers. "I was giving a lecture at the time. On the fascinating subject of reanimation through culinary means, as it happens."

Morty's eyebrows shot up. "Reanimation through... cooking?"

"Indeed," Dr. Frankie nodded. "A rather niche field, I'll admit."

She turned the tablet towards Morty. On the screen, a video played. It showed Dr. Frankie, unmistakable in her dramatic attire, gesticulating at a podium. A time stamp in the corner matched the estimated time of Ima's murder.

Morty squinted at the footage. "This could be doctored," he mused, more to himself than to Dr. Frankie.

"Your skepticism is admirable," she replied. "But perhaps this will convince you."

She swiped to another video. This one showed the same lecture hall, but from a different angle. In the corner, a digital clock ticked away the minutes.

"This is from the building's security feed," Dr. Frankie explained. "I obtained it through... shall we say, unofficial channels."

Morty watched as the clock in the video synced perfectly with Dr. Frankie's movements on stage. It seemed genuine, but doubt still gnawed at him.

"And where exactly was this lecture?" he asked.

"The Miskatonic Culinary Institute," Dr. Frankie replied smoothly. "About three hours from Hollow Creek. I drove back immediately after, which is why I arrived on the scene so quickly."

Morty's mind raced. The alibi seemed solid, but something still felt off. He couldn't shake the feeling that Dr. Frankie knew more than she was letting on.

"Well, Doc," he said finally, "it looks like you've got your bases covered. But I've got to ask – why go to all this trouble? Why not just tell the police?"

Dr. Frankie's green eyes glittered. "Because, my dear Mortimer, the police in this town are about as useful as a chocolate teapot. And besides," she leaned in close, her voice dropping to a conspiratorial whisper, "where's the fun in that?"

Morty couldn't help but chuckle. Dr. Frankie's dark humor resonated with his own macabre sensibilities. He studied her face, searching for any sign of deception.

"Alright, Doc," he said, running a hand through his wild hair. "I'm still not entirely convinced, but I'm willing to give you the benefit of the doubt."

Dr. Frankie's lips curved into a subtle smile. "That's all I ask, Mortimer."

Morty sighed, his portly frame sagging slightly. "So, where do we go from here? I'm not exactly a detective, you know. My expertise lies more in creating edible eyeballs than solving murders."

"That's precisely why we make an excellent team," Dr. Frankie replied, her voice smooth as silk. "Your unique perspective could be invaluable. And let's not forget, you have a vested interest in clearing your name."

Morty nodded, his mind already conjuring up gruesome culinary metaphors for their investigation. "Well, I suppose we could slice into this mystery like a perfectly roasted pumpkin."

Dr. Frankie's eyes glimmered with amusement. "Indeed. And I assure you, Mortimer, I am fully committed to helping you clear your name and solve this case. Your trust in me won't be misplaced."

Morty felt a wave of relief wash over him. Despite his lingering doubts, having an ally in this predicament was comforting. "I appreciate that, Doc. Really, I do. It's been a bit lonely being the town's prime suspect."

"I can imagine," Dr. Frankie said, her tone softening. "But you're not alone anymore. We'll get to the bottom of this, one clue at a time."

Morty's brow furrowed as he stroked his salt-and-pepper beard. "Alright, then. Let's start carving into this mystery. Who do you think we should interrogate first?"

Dr. Frankie tapped her long, pale fingers against her chin. "We should consider everyone who had access to the festival grounds that night. The vendors, the staff, even the performers."

"Don't forget the guests," Morty added, his eyes widening. "Ima Picky wasn't exactly beloved. Half the town probably wanted to stuff her like a jack-o'-lantern."

A dry chuckle escaped Dr. Frankie's lips. "Quite. We'll need to compile a list of potential suspects and their motives."

Morty's mind raced, thoughts bubbling like a witch's cauldron. He paced the room, his heavy footsteps echoing. "There's something else that's been gnawing at me like a hungry zombie."

Dr. Frankie raised an eyebrow. "Oh?"

"Mayor Candy Corn," Morty spat, his jovial demeanor souring. "That sugar-coated snake has been meddling in the investigation. I can feel it in my bones."

"Ah, yes. Our illustrious mayor," Dr. Frankie mused. "His interference is... concerning."

Morty's fists clenched. "Concerning? It's downright terrifying! If we don't expose his corruption soon, he'll turn the Hollow Creek Halloween Festival into his own personal candy shop."

Dr. Frankie nodded solemnly. "I share your concerns, Mortimer. Mayor Candy Corn's influence runs deep in this town. We'll need solid evidence to challenge him."

Morty's eyes gleamed with determination. "Then that's what we'll get. I won't let him ruin Halloween for Hollow Creek. It's time we peeled back his sugary facade and revealed the rotten core beneath."

Dr. Frankie Stein's piercing green eyes narrowed, a spark of intrigue igniting within them. She leaned forward, her voice dropping to a conspiratorial whisper. "I believe I have a solution to our predicament, Mortimer."

Morty paused his pacing, his wild hair seeming to crackle with anticipation. "I'm all ears, Doc. What's cooking in that brilliant mind of yours?"

A sly smile played across Dr. Frankie's pale lips. "We have an extensive network of contacts and informants throughout Hollow Creek. It's time we put them to use."

Morty's eyebrows shot up, disappearing beneath his unruly mop of hair. "Informants? You mean like spies?"

"In a manner of speaking," Dr. Frankie replied, her tone measured. "These are individuals who owe me favors or have a vested interest in maintaining the integrity of our beloved Halloween festivities."

Morty's mind whirred with possibilities. "So, we send them out to gather dirt on Mayor Candy Corn?"

"Precisely," Dr. Frankie nodded. "But we must proceed with caution. The mayor has eyes and ears everywhere. Our movements must be as discreet as a ghost in the night."

Morty rubbed his chin thoughtfully, his chef's instincts kicking in. "We need to cook up a plan that's both sweet and savory. Something that'll satisfy our hunger for justice without leaving a bad taste in anyone's mouth."

Dr. Frankie's eyes glimmered with approval. "Indeed. I propose we divide our efforts. While our contacts gather information on the mayor, we continue investigating other potential suspects in Ima's murder."

Morty snapped his fingers, his face lighting up like a jack-o'-lantern. "That's brilliant! We'll be killing two bats with one stone!"

"Quite," Dr. Frankie agreed, a hint of amusement in her voice. "Now, let's discuss the specifics of our plan..."

As they delved into the details, Morty felt a mix of excitement and unease bubbling in his stomach like an experimental potion. Dr. Frankie's plan was intricate, weaving a web of informants and strategic moves that impressed even his culinary creativity.

"So, we'll meet back here at the stroke of midnight?" Morty asked, his voice hushed despite the empty restaurant.

Dr. Frankie nodded, her green eyes glinting in the dim light. "The witching hour seems appropriate, don't you think? We'll compare notes and plot our next move."

Morty's fingers drummed nervously on the table. "And you're sure your contacts can be trusted?"

"As sure as death and taxes," Dr. Frankie replied with a wry smile. "But I understand your caution, Morty. Trust is a rare commodity these days."

He studied her face, searching for any sign of deception. Her calm demeanor revealed nothing. Morty's doubts gnawed at him like hungry ghosts.

"I appreciate your help, Dr. Frankie," he said carefully. "But I hope you understand that I need to keep my eyes open. This whole situation is as sticky as a caramel apple."

Dr. Frankie's expression softened. "I wouldn't expect anything less from you, Morty. Skepticism is a chef's best friend when testing new recipes. Apply that same discernment to our partnership."

Morty nodded, feeling a mix of relief and lingering suspicion. As they parted ways, he resolved to watch Dr. Frankie's every move, ready to reassess their alliance at the slightest hint of betrayal.

Morty stood alone in The Ghoulish Gourmet, the silence pressing in around him like a thick fog. The emptiness of his beloved restaurant, usually bustling with laughter and the clinking of plates, now felt oppressive. He moved through the shadowy dining room, his footsteps echoing hollowly.

At the bar, he poured himself a glass of pumpkin spice whiskey, a specialty he'd concocted for the Halloween season. The familiar scent of cinnamon and nutmeg wafted up, momentarily grounding him. Morty took a deep swig, savoring the warmth as it spread through his chest.

"What a mess you've gotten yourself into this time, old boy," he muttered to his reflection in the mirrored back bar. His wild hair seemed even more frazzled than usual, matching his frayed nerves.

Morty's mind raced, replaying the events of the past few days. The discovery of Ima Picky's body, stuffed like a macabre turducken into one of his prized jack-o'-lanterns. The accusatory glares from townsfolk who once adored his culinary creations. Mayor Candy Corn's thinly veiled threats. And now, this tenuous alliance with the enigmatic Dr. Frankie Stein.

He took another sip of whiskey, mulling over his next moves. "I've got to clear my name," Morty declared to the empty room. "But how to serve up justice without getting charbroiled myself?"

The chef's eyes fell on a framed photo behind the bar – himself as a young apprentice, standing proudly next to his grandmother. Her words echoed in his memory: "Remember, Mortimer, the key to any great dish is balance. Too much of one ingredient, and the whole recipe falls apart."

Morty straightened his spine, a spark of determination igniting in his chest. "Balance," he repeated. "I need to keep my wits sharp and my knives sharper. Trust, but verify. And above all, stay true to my own recipe for success."

He raised his glass in a solitary toast. "To uncovering the truth, Gran. May it be as sweet as your legendary pumpkin pie."

As Morty drained the last of his whiskey, a chill ran down his spine. The unmistakable feeling of being watched prickled at the back of his neck. He whirled around, scanning the darkened restaurant.

For a fleeting moment, he could have sworn he saw a shadowy figure dart past the front window. But when he blinked, there was nothing but the empty street beyond.

Morty's heart raced. Was his imagination playing tricks on him, or was there a very real danger lurking in the shadows of Hollow Creek?

With trembling hands, he reached for his phone to call Dr. Frankie. But as his fingers hovered over the keypad, he hesitated. Could he truly trust her? Or would reaching out now only place him in greater peril?

Taking a deep breath, Morty steeled himself. He had to face this challenge head-on, relying on his own instincts and skills. The truth was out there, waiting to be uncovered like the perfect blend of spices in a complex dish.

"Alright, Morty," he whispered to himself. "Time to cook up a plan that'll make even the toughest critics savor every bite."

With renewed resolve, Morty moved towards the kitchen. He had work to do before his midnight rendezvous with Dr. Frankie. And this time, he'd be prepared for whatever sinister ingredients fate might throw into his culinary mystery.

CHAPTER 9

Morty's office at The Ghoulish Gourmet was a cacophony of culinary chaos. Copper pots dangled precariously from the ceiling. Recipe books with ominous titles lined the shelves. In the center, a large oak desk groaned under the weight of paperwork and half-eaten experiments.

Morty drummed his fingers on the desk, his wild hair crackling with static. "Alright, my ghastly gourmands, let's stir this cauldron of suspicion we've got brewing about Peter Parasol."

Dr. Frankie Stein leaned against a bookshelf, her piercing green eyes narrowed. "The evidence we have is circumstantial at best. We need more."

Willow Shadowmoon nodded, her violet eyes distant. "I sense a darkness around him, but it's... elusive."

Morty chuckled darkly. "Well, we can't serve up justice without a proper recipe, can we? We need to gather more ingredients - I mean, evidence."

"Agreed," Dr. Frankie said. "But how do we proceed without alerting Peter?"

Morty's eyes lit up with mischievous glee. "I might have a few tricks up my sleeve. Or should I say, under my chef's hat?"

Willow raised an eyebrow. "Do tell, Morty. What devilish plan are you cooking up?"

"I've got connections all over town," Morty explained, rubbing his hands together. "From the butcher to the baker to the candlestick maker. They hear things, see things. I can ask them to keep an ear to the ground about Peter's interactions with our dear departed Ima Picky."

Dr. Frankie nodded approvingly. "Clever. And while you're doing that, I can analyze any physical evidence we can find. There might be clues we've overlooked."

Morty grinned, revealing slightly pointed canines. "Now we're cooking with ghost pepper! But we'll need to be discreet. Can't have Peter getting wind of our little investigation."

"Leave that to me," Willow said, her voice soft but determined. "I can... observe Peter without him knowing. My methods are... unconventional, but effective."

Morty clapped his hands together, sending a small shock through the air. "Excellent! We'll gather our evidence, then confront Peter with a banquet of proof he can't possibly deny."

Dr. Frankie's lips curled into a rare smile. "I must admit, Morty, your enthusiasm for this is both admirable and slightly disturbing."

"Why, thank you, my dear doctor!" Morty beamed. "Now, let's get cooking. We've got a murderer to catch, and I've got a new 'Guilty as Sin' soufflé to perfect for the occasion!"

As they filed out of the office, a stray breeze caught one of Morty's recipe cards. It fluttered to the floor, revealing a hastily scribbled note: "Ima Picky - secret ingredient?" The card lay there, unnoticed, as the door swung shut behind them.

Willow Shadowmoon closed her eyes, her long, dark lashes fluttering against her pale cheeks. The air around her seemed to shimmer, as if reality itself bent to her will.

"I sense... turmoil," she murmured, her soft voice taking on an otherworldly quality. "Peter's aura is a maelstrom of fear, resentment, and... something darker."

Morty leaned forward, his wild hair crackling with static electricity. "Can you dig deeper, Willow? We need more than just vibes to nail this ghostly gourmet."

Willow's brow furrowed in concentration. "I'm trying to pierce the veil, but there's resistance. It's as if Peter's very soul is cowering, hiding from my sight."

Dr. Frankie Stein rolled her eyes, barely suppressing a scoff. "Perhaps we should focus on more tangible evidence?"

Morty shot her a reproachful look. "Now, now, doctor. In Hollow Creek, we embrace all forms of investigation – scientific and supernatural alike."

Willow's eyes snapped open, their violet hue unnaturally bright. "I've glimpsed something. A memory, perhaps. Peter, trembling before Ima Picky, her words lashing him like whips. The air thick with the scent of... truffles?"

Morty's bushy eyebrows shot up. "Truffles, you say? Interesting... very interesting indeed."

As Willow regained her composure, Morty pulled out his phone, fingers flying over the screen. "Time to put my connections to good use," he muttered.

"Who are you contacting?" Dr. Frankie asked, curiosity overcoming her skepticism.

Morty's eyes twinkled mischievously. "Oh, just a few culinary cohorts, some gastronomic gossips, and perhaps a sous-chef or two with loose lips."

He fired off a series of texts, each more cryptic than the last. "Zombie Bob, got any dirt on Parasol? ... Vampira, darling, heard any juicy rumors about Ima's last days? ... Werewolf Warren, sniffed out any strange behavior at the Picky Palace lately?"

As the messages whooshed away, Morty looked up, a devious grin spreading across his face. "And now, my friends, we wait for the pot to simmer. Something tells me we're about to uncover a recipe for murder most foul."

Dr. Frankie Stein stood in Ima Picky's office, her piercing green eyes scanning the room. The scent of expensive perfume lingered, mingling with the faint odor of decay. She snapped on a pair of latex gloves, the sound echoing in the eerie silence.

"Let's see what secrets you were hiding, Ms. Picky," she murmured, her voice cool and clinical.

She moved to the ornate desk, its surface polished to a mirror sheen. Carefully, she began rifling through drawers, her movements precise and methodical. Papers rustled beneath her fingers.

"Interesting," Dr. Stein muttered, holding up a stack of letters. "Correspondence between Ima and Peter. Quite vitriolic, I must say."

She pulled out her phone, snapping photos of each page. The camera clicked rhythmically as she documented the evidence.

Meanwhile, in another part of Hollow Creek, Willow Shadowmoon sat cross-legged on a plush cushion. Candles flickered around her, casting dancing shadows on the walls. She closed her violet eyes, her breathing slow and steady.

"Spirit guides," she intoned, her voice barely above a whisper, "show me the truth of Peter Parasol's heart."

The air around her seemed to thicken, charged with unseen energy. Willow's brow furrowed in concentration.

"I see... I see a man, cowering in fear," she murmured. "Anger, so much anger, buried deep. And... guilt. Oh, such crushing guilt."

Her eyes flew open, wide with shock. "By the spirits," she gasped, "what have you done, Peter Parasol?"

Morty's office buzzed with activity. Papers rustled. Phones chimed. The portly chef paced, his wild hair even more disheveled than usual.

"What've you got for me, Bonesy?" Morty barked into his phone, his free hand twirling a wooden spoon like a baton.

A gravelly voice crackled through the speaker. "Boss, you ain't gonna believe this. Remember that fancy shindig at the Hollow Creek Country Club last month?"

Morty's bushy eyebrows shot up. "The one where Ima Picky made that poor sous chef cry?"

"Bingo. Well, turns out our boy Peter was there too. And let's just say, Ima didn't exactly roll out the red carpet for him."

Morty's grip tightened on the spoon. "Spill it, Bonesy. What happened?"

"Witnesses say Ima spent the whole night parading Peter around like a show pony. Made him fetch her drinks, carry her purse. Even had him taste-test everything before she'd eat it."

Morty winced. "Ouch. Talk about humiliation on a silver platter."

"That ain't all, boss. When Peter accidentally spilled some wine on her dress, she went ballistic. Called him every name in the book, right there in front of everyone."

Morty's face darkened. "Poor guy. No wonder he always looks like he's expecting a slap."

He jotted down notes, his handwriting a chaotic scrawl. "Any photos from that night, Bonesy?"

"You bet. Sending 'em over now."

Morty's phone pinged. He scrolled through the images, each one a snapshot of Peter's misery. The chef's jovial face twisted with sympathy.

"Thanks, Bonesy. You've outdone yourself."

He hung up, staring at the evidence before him. "Oh, Peter," he muttered, "what a tangled web we weave."

Across town, Dr. Frankie Stein hunched over her laptop, her brow furrowed in concentration. Stacks of newspapers and printouts surrounded her like a paper fortress.

She clicked through Ima Picky's articles, her eyes darting back and forth. "Interesting," she murmured, tapping a long finger against her chin.

Her gaze landed on a particularly scathing review of The Ghoulish Gourmet. "Morty's culinary monstrosities are an affront to good taste," she read aloud, her voice tinged with amusement.

But as she cross-referenced the article with her gathered evidence, something didn't add up. She pulled up a photo from that night, squinting at the details.

"Wait a minute," she muttered, zooming in on a figure in the background. It was Peter Parasol, his face a mask of misery as he trailed behind Ima.

Dr. Stein's eyes widened. "She wrote this review before she even tasted the food," she realized, her voice filled with shock and a hint of triumph.

She quickly typed up her findings, her fingers flying over the keyboard. As she worked, a chill ran down her spine. The pieces were falling into place, and the picture they formed was darker than she'd imagined.

Meanwhile, Willow Shadowmoon sat cross-legged on the floor of her dim, incense-filled room. Her eyes were closed, hands resting lightly on her knees.

She took a deep breath, centering herself. "Show me the truth," she whispered, her voice barely audible.

Suddenly, her eyes flew open, revealing a swirl of violet. Images flashed through her mind, rapid and intense.

Peter Parasol, his face contorted with anger. Ima Picky, her laughter cruel and mocking. A swirl of emotions - humiliation, rage, and... something else.

Willow gasped, her body trembling. "By the spirits," she murmured, her voice shaky.

She scrambled to her feet, nearly knocking over a crystal ball in her haste. She had to tell Morty and Dr. Stein immediately.

As she rushed out, her robes billowing behind her, she couldn't shake the intensity of what she'd sensed. The connection between Peter and Ima was more complex than they'd imagined.

At The Ghoulish Gourmet, Morty paced his office, muttering to himself. "What's taking them so long?" he grumbled, eyeing the clock.

Just then, Dr. Stein burst through the door, her usually calm demeanor replaced by excitement. "Morty, you won't believe what I've found!"

Before she could continue, Willow appeared, slightly out of breath. "I have urgent news," she announced, her eyes wild.

Morty looked between them, his bushy eyebrows raised. "Ladies, ladies," he said, holding up his hands. "One at a time. Let's start with you, Doc."

Dr. Stein laid out her findings, pointing to the discrepancies in Ima's reviews. Morty's face darkened as he listened.

"That sneaky little..." he growled, trailing off. "But why would she do that?"

Willow stepped forward, her voice soft but intense. "I believe I can shed some light on that," she said, her eyes meeting Morty's.

Morty's office phone rang, cutting through the tension. He snatched it up, his face a mix of anticipation and dread.

"Graves speaking," he barked. His eyes widened. "Jack? Perfect timing."

Dr. Stein and Willow exchanged glances as Morty listened, nodding occasionally.

"Listen, Jack," Morty said, his voice lowering. "We've got some serious evidence against Peter Parasol. We need to confront him, and we need you there."

A pause. Morty's brow furrowed.

"No, not another false alarm. This is the real deal." He drummed his fingers on the desk. "Meet us at his place in an hour. And Jack? Bring your badge."

He hung up, turning to the women. "Ladies, we're heading to Peter's. Jack's meeting us there."

Dr. Stein raised an eyebrow. "Are you sure involving Jack is wise? His tendency to jump to conclusions could complicate matters."

Morty shrugged, grabbing his coat. "We need this by the book. Besides, Jack's heart's in the right place, even if his brain takes detours."

Willow nodded sagely. "The spirits approve. Jack's presence will bring balance to our confrontation."

They gathered their evidence and headed out. The drive to Peter's was tense, each lost in their thoughts.

As they pulled up to Peter's house, they spotted Jack's patrol car. The detective stood beside it, his tie askew and hair ruffled.

"Ready for this?" Morty asked, his hand on the car door.

Dr. Stein nodded grimly. "As ready as one can be to accuse a man of murder."

Willow closed her eyes briefly. "The energy here is... turbulent. We must proceed with caution."

They exited the car, approaching Jack. The detective's face was a mix of confusion and determination.

"Alright, Morty," Jack said, scratching his head. "Let's get to the bottom of this pickle barrel."

Morty sighed. It was going to be a long night.

Morty approached Peter Parasol's front door, his heart pounding. The porch light flickered, casting eerie shadows. He raised his hand and knocked firmly.

Shuffling sounds came from inside. Morty glanced back at his companions, their faces tense in the dim light.

The door creaked open. Peter Parasol stood there, his thin frame hunched, eyes darting nervously between them.

"Mr. Parasol," Morty said, trying to keep his voice steady. "We need to talk."

Peter's adam's apple bobbed as he swallowed hard. "W-what about?"

Morty took a deep breath. "About Ima Picky's murder."

Peter's eyes widened, his face paling further. "I-I don't know anything about that."

"May we come in?" Dr. Stein interjected, her tone professional but firm.

Peter hesitated, then stepped back, allowing them entry.

Inside, the living room was cluttered, stacks of food magazines everywhere. Morty's culinary instincts noted the faint smell of burnt toast.

"Mr. Parasol," Morty began, "we have evidence that suggests your involvement in Ima's death."

Peter's hands trembled. "That's... that's impossible. I would never..."

Morty pulled out a folder. "We have witness accounts of Ima mistreating you publicly. And financial records showing large withdrawals from your account just before her death."

Peter's face contorted. "She... she was cruel, yes. But I didn't kill her!"

Dr. Stein stepped forward. "We found your fingerprints on the murder weapon, Peter."

Peter's eyes darted around the room, like a cornered animal. Morty felt a pang of sympathy, despite everything.

"It's not what you think," Peter whispered, his voice cracking. "I... I was there, but..."

Morty leaned in. "But what, Peter? What happened?"

Peter's resolve crumbled. Tears welled in his eyes. "She was going to ruin everything. My career, my life. I just wanted her to stop."

The room fell silent. Morty's mind raced. They were close to the truth, but something still felt off.

Willow's eyes narrowed, her psychic senses tingling. "There's more, isn't there, Peter? Something you're holding back."

Peter's gaze dropped to the floor. His shoulders slumped. "I... I didn't mean for it to happen. It was an accident."

Detective Jack O'Lantern stepped forward, fumbling with his handcuffs. "Well, that's enough for me. Peter Parasol, you're under arrest for the murder of Ima Picky."

"Wait," Morty interjected, holding up a hand. Something didn't add up. "Peter, what exactly was an accident?"

Peter's eyes darted between them, his breath coming in short gasps. "I confronted her, yes. But I didn't kill her. We argued, and she... she slipped. Hit her head on the corner of her desk. I panicked. I tried to help, but..."

Dr. Stein's brow furrowed. "That doesn't explain the murder weapon with your fingerprints."

"I picked it up!" Peter blurted. "After she fell. I didn't know what to do. I thought... I thought if I made it look like a robbery gone wrong..."

Morty exchanged glances with his companions. The pieces were falling into place, but not quite as they'd expected.

"Jack," Morty said quietly, "I think we need to reconsider our approach here."

The detective scratched his head. "But he just confessed!"

"To manslaughter, perhaps," Dr. Stein corrected. "Not premeditated murder."

Willow closed her eyes, concentrating. "I sense... remorse. Fear. But not the darkness of a cold-blooded killer."

Peter collapsed onto his couch, burying his face in his hands. "I never meant for any of this to happen. I just wanted her to listen, to understand how her words were destroying people's lives."

Morty felt a mix of emotions swirling in his chest. Sympathy for Peter, frustration at the complexity of the situation, and a nagging feeling that there was still more to uncover.

"We need to take him in," Jack insisted, jingling his handcuffs.

"Agreed," Morty nodded. "But not as our murderer. As a material witness. We still have work to do."

CHAPTER 10

The town hall loomed before Morty, its Gothic spires piercing the gloomy sky. He adjusted his pumpkin-patterned tie and pushed through the heavy oak doors.

Mayor Candy Corn's office reeked of artificial sweetness. The mayor himself sat behind an ornate desk, his candy corn cufflinks glinting in the dim light.

"Ah, Mortimer! What brings you to my humble abode?" The mayor's voice oozed like syrup.

Morty's eyes narrowed. "Cut the act, Cornelius. I want answers about why you're trying to shut down my investigation."

The mayor's smile didn't waver. "My dear boy, you've got it all wrong. I'm simply looking out for our beloved Hollow Creek."

"By obstructing justice?" Morty's fists clenched at his sides.

Mayor Candy Corn tsked. "Such harsh words. I assure you, it's all a misunderstanding."

Morty slammed his palms on the desk. "No more games. You're involved in this murder cover-up, aren't you?"

The mayor's eyes hardened. "That's a grave accusation, Mortimer. I'd advise you to choose your next words carefully."

"Or what?" Morty leaned closer, the scent of pumpkin spice clinging to his clothes. "You'll add me to your list of victims?"

Mayor Candy Corn stood, his portly frame casting a shadow. "I've worked tirelessly for this town. I won't let some meddling chef ruin everything I've built."

Morty's laugh was as sharp as a butcher's knife. "Built on lies and corruption, you mean."

The tension crackled between them like static electricity in Morty's wild hair.

"You're in over your head, Graves," the mayor growled. "Back off now, while you still can."

Morty's mind raced. He was onto something big, he could feel it. But how deep did this conspiracy go?

"Never," Morty declared. "I'll expose you, Cornelius. Mark my words."

As he stormed out, Morty's determination solidified like gelatin in a mold. He'd need help to take down the mayor, but he wouldn't rest until justice was served.

Morty's footsteps echoed through Hollow Creek's twilight-drenched streets. His mind buzzed with the mayor's thinly veiled threats. He needed allies, and fast.

Dr. Frankie Stein's laboratory loomed ahead, a Gothic silhouette against the purpling sky. Morty rapped on the heavy oak door.

"Frankie! It's Morty. We need to talk."

The door creaked open. Frankie's piercing green eyes peered out.

"Morty? You look like you've seen a ghost."

He chuckled darkly. "Worse. Our esteemed mayor."

Inside, amid bubbling beakers and whirring contraptions, Morty recounted his confrontation. Frankie listened, her brow furrowing.

"This is grave indeed," she mused. "We'll need more than just science to unravel this mystery."

Morty nodded. "I know just who to call."

Minutes later, Willow Shadowmoon swept in, her robes rustling like autumn leaves.

"I sensed a disturbance in the ethereal plane," she intoned. "What darkness plagues our fair town?"

Morty filled her in, his hands gesticulating wildly. "We need a plan to expose Candy Corn's corruption."

Frankie tapped her chin. "Evidence is key. But how to obtain it without arousing suspicion?"

Willow's violet eyes glimmered. "Perhaps a séance to commune with the spirits of his past misdeeds?"

Morty suppressed a groan. "Let's start with something more... tangible."

As they brainstormed, Morty felt hope rising like yeast in warm dough. With these formidable allies by his side, even Mayor Candy Corn's saccharine facade would crumble.

The trio spent days scouring Hollow Creek's archives, poring over dusty ledgers and faded newspaper clippings. Morty's kitchen became their war room, scented with pumpkin spice and conspiracy.

"Look at this," Frankie muttered, pushing a document across the flour-dusted table. "A zoning change that benefited Candy Corn's brother-in-law."

Morty squinted at the fine print. "And conveniently bulldozed a historic cemetery. How ghoulishly fitting."

Willow's crystal pendant swung as she leaned in. "The spirits are restless. They whisper of more transgressions."

Piece by piece, they assembled a mosaic of Mayor Candy Corn's misdeeds. Embezzled funds. Rigged contracts. A trail of broken promises sticky as melted candy.

Morty's blood boiled hotter than his famous ghost pepper sauce. "We've got him cornered like a rat in a pumpkin patch."

But as they celebrated their progress over Morty's "Phantom Philly Cheesesteaks," a chill wind rattled the windows.

Frankie's phone buzzed. Her face paled. "My lab... there's been a break-in."

Across town, Mayor Candy Corn paced his office, sweat beading on his brow. He barked into his phone, "I don't care how you do it. Shut them down. Now."

He hung up, fingers trembling as he reached for his candy corn dispenser. The sweet kernels did little to quell the bitter taste of panic rising in his throat.

The next morning, Morty stepped out of his haunted house-themed food truck, only to find Officer Grimshaw leaning against the hood.

"Health inspection," Grimshaw growled, flashing a dubious badge.

Morty's eyebrow arched. "At 6 AM? How thoughtful."

As Grimshaw ransacked the truck, Morty's mind raced. He knew his kitchen was spotless, but this wasn't about cleanliness.

"Find any ghosts in the goulash?" Morty quipped, masking his unease.

Grimshaw sneered. "Keep joking, Graves. We're watching you."

Across town, Willow hurried down Main Street, her long hair whipping in the wind. She sensed a presence following her, dark and menacing. Ducking into an alley, she whispered an incantation, vanishing in a puff of lavender smoke just as another officer rounded the corner.

Dr. Frankie Stein, meanwhile, found herself cornered in her lab by two uniformed men.

"Gentlemen," she said coolly, "I assume you have a warrant?"

One officer stepped forward. "We have questions about your recent... experiments."

Frankie's mind whirred. She needed a distraction. Her eyes landed on a bubbling beaker.

"Of course," she smiled. "Let me just turn off this highly unstable compound..."

In one fluid motion, she knocked over the beaker. Harmless but impressive smoke filled the room, allowing her to slip away.

Later, the trio reconvened at Morty's apartment, breathless and shaken.

"They're closing in," Morty said, pacing. "We need irrefutable evidence."

Willow's eyes gleamed. "I have an idea. But it's risky."

Frankie leaned forward. "We're listening."

"A hidden camera," Willow explained. "In Candy Corn's office."

Morty grinned. "Now that's a recipe for justice I can get behind."

Morty's heart pounded as he crouched behind a hedge outside Town Hall. The night air was crisp, carrying the scent of fallen leaves. He peered at his watch, its face glowing faintly in the darkness.

"Any movement?" Dr. Frankie Stein's voice crackled through his earpiece.

"Negative," Morty whispered. "Our candy-coated culprit is still inside."

Across the street, Willow Shadowmoon sat in a parked car, her violet eyes fixed on the building's entrance. She twirled a crystal pendant between her fingers, its energy pulsing in sync with her anxiety.

"I sense a shift in the aether," Willow murmured. "He'll emerge soon."

Minutes ticked by, each second stretching like taffy. Morty's legs cramped, but he dared not move. Too much was at stake.

Suddenly, the Town Hall doors swung open. Mayor Candy Corn strutted out, his gaudy suit a beacon in the night.

"Showtime," Morty breathed.

As the mayor climbed into his car, Morty counted to ten. Then he sprinted across the lawn, ducking low. He reached the side entrance, fumbling with the lock pick Frankie had provided.

"Hurry," Frankie urged in his ear. "You've got three minutes before the night guard rounds the corner."

Morty's fingers trembled. The lock clicked. He slipped inside, heart thundering.

The hallways were dim, shadows lurking in every corner. Morty crept towards Candy Corn's office, wincing at each creak of the floorboards.

"Left, then right," Willow guided him. "The spirits are with you, Morty."

He reached the office door, sweat beading on his brow. Another lock to pick. Precious seconds ticked away.

"Two minutes," Frankie warned.

The lock yielded. Morty eased the door open, slipping inside. He fumbled for the hidden camera, tucked behind a garish painting of the mayor.

"Got it," he whispered triumphantly.

"One minute," Frankie's voice was tense. "Get out now, Morty."

He pocketed the camera and turned to leave. A floorboard groaned outside.

Morty froze. Footsteps approached.

"Hide!" Willow hissed.

Morty dove under the mayor's desk, his heart pounding like a jackhammer. The door creaked open. Heavy footsteps entered.

"Just a quick check," the night guard mumbled.

Morty held his breath, praying the guard wouldn't look too closely. Seconds felt like hours.

Finally, the footsteps retreated. The door clicked shut.

"Coast is clear," Frankie whispered in his ear. "Move!"

Morty scrambled out, legs wobbling. He slipped into the hallway, adrenaline coursing through his veins.

Outside, the cool night air hit his face. He sprinted across the lawn, clutching the camera like a lifeline.

"I've got it," he panted, sliding into Frankie's waiting car.

Willow grinned from the backseat. "Let's see what skeletons our dear mayor has in his closet."

They huddled around the tiny screen, watching with growing horror as Mayor Candy Corn's corruption unfolded before their eyes.

"This is worse than we thought," Frankie muttered.

Morty's jaw clenched. "Time to serve up some just desserts."

The next morning, Hollow Creek's town square buzzed with anticipation. Morty stood on the makeshift stage, flanked by Frankie and Willow. A projector loomed behind them.

Mayor Candy Corn swaggered up, his candy corn tie glinting in the sun. "What's all this hullabaloo about, Graves? Another one of your spooky food festivals?"

Morty's eyes narrowed. "Oh, it's a festival alright. A festival of truth."

He nodded to Frankie, who hit play. The mayor's smug grin faltered as his own voice filled the square, detailing bribes and cover-ups.

The crowd gasped. Whispers turned to shouts of outrage.

"This is preposterous!" Candy Corn sputtered, his face turning as red as a blood orange. "Clearly doctored footage!"

Morty stepped forward, his voice ringing out. "The only thing doctored here is your public image, Mr. Mayor. Your reign of corruption ends now."

The mayor's eyes darted, seeking an escape. Finding none, he plastered on a sickly-sweet smile.

"My dear citizens," he began, "I can explain. These actions, while regrettable, were all for the greater good of Hollow Creek."

Boos erupted from the crowd. Someone threw a rotten pumpkin, narrowly missing the mayor's head.

"Greater good?" Morty scoffed. "The only thing you've been looking out for is your own bottom line."

Candy Corn's facade crumbled. "You don't understand the pressures of this office! I had no choice!"

"There's always a choice," Willow chimed in, her voice cutting through the chaos. "And you chose greed over your duty to this town."

The crowd's anger swelled. Chants of "Resign! Resign!" filled the air.

Morty watched as the mayor's shoulders slumped, defeat etched on his face. For a moment, he almost felt pity. Almost.

"I think it's time you hung up that candy corn tie for good, Mr. Mayor," Morty said, his voice low but firm. "Hollow Creek deserves better."

As the police arrived to escort Candy Corn away, Morty couldn't help but wonder: what other secrets lurked beneath Hollow Creek's festive surface?

The following days passed in a whirlwind of activity. Morty watched with a mixture of pride and exhaustion as justice unfolded across Hollow Creek. The corrupt law enforcement officers were led away in handcuffs, their badges tarnished beyond repair.

"Never thought I'd see the day," Morty muttered, stirring a bubbling cauldron of his famous pumpkin soup.

Dr. Frankie Stein entered the kitchen, her lab coat swishing. "The town's abuzz with talk of change. It's... refreshing."

Morty nodded, a wry smile tugging at his lips. "Like a breath of fresh air after a century in a crypt, eh?"

"Your metaphors never fail to disgust and delight, Morty," Frankie replied, her green eyes twinkling.

Willow Shadowmoon materialized beside them, her dark hair seeming to float on an unseen breeze. "The spirits are restless. They sense a shift in the cosmic balance."

Morty raised an eyebrow. "That's just my chili, Willow. Extra beans today."

The three friends shared a laugh, the sound echoing through the kitchen. But beneath the levity, a current of seriousness ran deep.

"We've won a battle," Frankie said, her tone sobering. "But the war for Hollow Creek's soul is far from over."

Morty nodded, his wild hair crackling with static electricity. "Agreed. We've peeled back one layer of this onion, but who knows what other rot lies beneath?"

Willow's violet eyes flashed. "We must remain vigilant. The veil between right and wrong is thin in this town."

"Then it's settled," Morty declared, raising his wooden spoon like a sword. "We continue our crusade for justice, one spooky dish at a time!"

As they clinked their mismatched mugs together, Morty couldn't shake the feeling that their greatest challenge still lay ahead. But with friends like these by his side, he was ready to face whatever Hollow Creek might throw at them next.

Morty wiped his hands on his apron, adorned with dancing skeletons. He surveyed the bustling kitchen of The Ghoulish Gourmet. Pots bubbled ominously. Knives flashed. Bella Notte, his sous chef, pirouetted between stations with balletic grace.

"Bella, my ghoul Friday! How's the Zombie Ziti coming along?" Morty called out.

Bella's eyes widened. "It's, um, almost ready, Chef. Just need to add the final... brains."

Morty chuckled. "Remember, we want them al dente, not mushy. No one likes overcooked cerebellum!"

As Bella nodded nervously, Morty's thoughts drifted to recent events. The town was still reeling from Mayor Candy Corn's downfall. But something nagged at him. A missing piece of the puzzle.

His musings were interrupted by a commotion at the kitchen door. Detective Jack O'Lantern burst in, tie askew and hair wilder than usual.

"Morty! We've got a situation!" Jack exclaimed, nearly tripping over a stray pumpkin.

Morty raised an eyebrow. "Jack, unless you're here to sample our new 'Corpse au Vin,' the kitchen's off-limits."

Jack shook his head frantically. "No time for culinary puns! There's been another murder!"

The kitchen fell silent. Even the bubbling pots seemed to hold their breath.

Morty's face darkened. "Where?"

"The old cemetery," Jack replied. "And get this – the victim was found inside Mayor Candy Corn's family mausoleum!"

Morty's mind raced. The Mayor's mausoleum? This couldn't be a coincidence.

"Any leads?" Morty asked, already reaching for his coat.

Jack fumbled with his notepad. "Well, uh, we found some strange symbols carved into the walls. And a half-eaten corn dog."

Morty groaned. "Jack, that's your corn dog. It's sticking out of your pocket."

The detective looked down, sheepish. "Oh. Right. But the symbols are real!"

Morty turned to Bella. "Hold down the fort, my apprentice of the arcane arts. I've got a date with death."

As they left, Bella called out, "But Chef, what about the Séance Soufflé?"

Morty paused at the door. "If it falls, just tell the customers it's supposed to do that. Call it 'Sunken Spirit Surprise!'"

With that, Morty and Jack headed for the cemetery, unaware that this new murder would plunge them into a web of secrets far darker than anything they'd faced before. And somewhere in the shadows, a figure watched, waiting for the perfect moment to strike.

CHAPTER 11

The Ghoulish Gourmet's kitchen crackled with tension. Morty's wild hair stood on end as he paced, spatula in hand.

"We're missing something," he muttered, tapping the utensil against his palm. "Ima Picky's past is like a perfectly prepared soufflé - one wrong move and it all falls apart."

Dr. Frankie Stein arched an eyebrow. "An apt metaphor, Morty. Though I'd argue her secrets are more akin to a house of cards."

Willow Shadowmoon's violet eyes gleamed in the dim light. "Perhaps we should consult the spirits for guidance?"

Morty shook his head. "No offense, Willow, but we need cold, hard facts. Not ethereal whispers."

"The spirits can provide valuable insights," Willow protested, her flowing robes rustling as she leaned forward.

"I'm sure they can," Morty said, his tone softening. "But right now, we need to focus on what we know."

Dr. Frankie Stein nodded, her silver-streaked hair catching the light. "Agreed. Let's review the facts."

Morty grabbed a nearby mixing bowl, dumping in imaginary ingredients as he spoke. "We know Ima was involved in the Halloween Festival incident. We know it had a major impact on the town. But we don't know why or how."

"It's like trying to bake a cake without knowing all the ingredients," he added, furiously whisking the empty bowl.

Dr. Frankie Stein's lips quirked. "Another culinary metaphor? You're on a roll today, Morty."

Morty grinned, but it quickly faded. He set down the bowl, his expression hardening with determination. "We need to uncover the truth. For the town's sake."

"And for your own, I suspect," Dr. Frankie Stein said softly.

Morty nodded, his normally jovial face serious. "Hollow Creek is my home. These people are my family. If Ima's actions hurt them, I need to know why."

Willow reached out, placing a comforting hand on Morty's arm. "We're with you, Morty. Whatever it takes."

"Indeed," Dr. Frankie Stein agreed. "Though I hope it doesn't come to anything too drastic. I'd hate to see your culinary talents go to waste in prison."

Morty chuckled despite himself. "Don't worry, Doc. I'll save my knife skills for the kitchen."

Dr. Frankie Stein's piercing green eyes narrowed in thought. "We need concrete evidence. Perhaps..." She paused, tapping a long finger against her chin. "Ima's home might hold the answers we seek."

Morty's eyebrows shot up. "Break into Ima Picky's house? That's a recipe for disaster!"

"Not breaking in," Dr. Frankie corrected, a hint of amusement in her voice. "Investigating. There must be records, documents, something tangible linking her to the festival incident."

Willow leaned forward, excitement glimmering in her eyes. "Old newspapers, diaries, photographs - anything could be a clue!"

Morty hesitated, his mind racing. It felt wrong, invasive. But the need for answers burned within him. "You really think we'll find something?"

"In my experience," Dr. Frankie said, her voice low and enigmatic, "everyone leaves traces of their past. Even those as meticulous as Ima Picky."

Decision made, Morty nodded firmly. "Alright, let's do it. But we need to be careful. Ima's got a tongue sharper than my best filleting knife."

As they gathered their things, a mix of anticipation and trepidation filled the air. Morty's heart pounded. What secrets would they uncover in Ima's lair? He only hoped the truth wouldn't be more bitter than even Ima's harshest critiques.

The trio stood before Ima Picky's Victorian-style home, its weathered facade looming ominously in the fading twilight. Morty suppressed a shudder. The house seemed to glare at them, windows like accusing eyes.

"Charming place," Dr. Frankie remarked dryly. "Very... welcoming."

Willow's violet eyes darted nervously. "The energy here is... unsettling. Like a veil of secrets."

Morty swallowed hard. "Let's just get this over with."

They approached the front door. Morty's hand trembled as he reached for the knob. To his surprise, it turned easily.

"Unlocked?" he whispered. "That's... convenient."

"Or a trap," Dr. Frankie muttered.

The door creaked open, revealing a dimly lit interior. Musty air assaulted their noses. Morty fumbled for a light switch.

"Wait!" Willow hissed. "What if someone sees?"

Dr. Frankie produced a small flashlight. "We'll have to make do with this."

They crept inside. Shadows danced across antique furniture and faded wallpaper. Morty's chef's intuition screamed that something was off.

"Where do we start?" he asked.

Dr. Frankie's eyes gleamed in the dim light. "Bedroom. Study. Anywhere she might keep personal items."

They split up, agreeing to meet back in fifteen minutes. Morty found himself in what appeared to be Ima's study. Bookshelves lined the walls. He ran a finger along the spines, squinting at titles.

"'The Art of Criticism'... 'Perfecting Your Palate'..." he muttered. "Nothing out of the ordinary."

A desk drawer caught his eye. Morty hesitated, then slowly pulled it open. Inside lay a leather-bound journal. His heart raced as he flipped it open.

Footsteps approached. Morty whirled around, nearly dropping the journal.

"Find anything?" Dr. Frankie asked, entering the room.

Morty held up the journal. "Maybe. You?"

She shook her head. "Nothing concrete yet. Willow's still upstairs."

A muffled thud echoed from above. They froze, exchanging alarmed glances.

"Willow?" Morty called softly.

No response.

Morty and Dr. Frankie rushed upstairs, their footsteps muffled by the plush carpet. They found Willow in Ima's bedroom, her face pale in the flashlight's beam.

"What happened?" Morty hissed.

Willow pointed a shaking finger at the wall. "I... I leaned against it and... it moved."

Dr. Frankie approached, running her hands along the floral wallpaper. Her fingers caught on a slight protrusion. With a soft click, a hidden door swung open.

"A secret room," Morty breathed. "Of course Ima would have one."

They peered inside. The beam of the flashlight revealed stacks of boxes and file cabinets.

"Jackpot," Dr. Frankie murmured.

They entered cautiously. Morty's pulse quickened as he opened the nearest box. Inside were dozens of photographs, all featuring the same event - the Hollow Creek Halloween Festival.

"Look at these," he said, holding up a handful. "They're all from different years, but... something's off."

Dr. Frankie leaned in, squinting. "The people. They look... scared."

Willow rifled through another box, pulling out newspaper clippings. "'Local Business Shuttered After Festival Disaster'... 'Mysterious Illness Strikes Festival-Goers'..."

Morty's stomach churned. "These go back decades. What was Ima doing?"

Dr. Frankie opened a file cabinet, extracting a thick folder. Her eyes widened as she scanned its contents. "Letters. Threatening letters. To festival organizers, local officials... even the mayor."

"From Ima?" Willow asked.

Dr. Frankie nodded grimly. "All signed with her signature acerbic wit."

Morty slumped against the wall, his mind reeling. "She wasn't just reviewing the festival. She was... sabotaging it. For years."

"But why?" Willow wondered.

A floorboard creaked outside the room. They froze, hearts pounding.

"Did you hear that?" Morty whispered.

Morty's heart raced as he stared at the incriminating evidence scattered around them. His hands trembled slightly as he picked up another photograph. The smiling faces of festival-goers from years past seemed to mock him now.

"I can't believe it," he muttered, his voice thick with emotion. "All these years, we thought Ima was just a cranky food critic. But this... this is something else entirely."

Dr. Frankie's usually calm demeanor was shaken. Her green eyes flashed with a mix of anger and disbelief as she pored over the threatening letters. "The level of malice here is... disturbing," she said, her voice barely above a whisper.

Willow hugged herself, her violet eyes wide with shock. "I'm sensing so much negative energy in this room. It's overwhelming."

Morty ran a hand through his wild hair, causing it to crackle with static. "Guys, do you realize what this means for our investigation? We're not just dealing with a simple murder anymore. This goes back decades."

Dr. Frankie nodded grimly. "Indeed. The implications are far-reaching. Ima's actions have affected not just the festival, but the entire town."

"Think about it," Willow added, her voice trembling slightly. "How many businesses closed because of these 'disasters'? How many people left town? How many lives were ruined?"

Morty's mind raced, recalling all the changes Hollow Creek had undergone over the years. "The old bakery that shut down... the haunted hayride that never reopened... even my great-aunt's cauldron cake shop. They all closed after particularly bad festival reviews."

"It wasn't just reviews," Dr. Frankie said, holding up one of the letters. "These are practically declarations of war against the town itself."

Willow closed her eyes, swaying slightly. "I can feel the ripples of her actions spreading through time. It's like... a dark web, touching everything in Hollow Creek."

Morty slumped against the wall, feeling the weight of their discovery. "We've got to do something. We can't let this continue."

Dr. Frankie's eyes narrowed with determination. "Agreed. But we need to be careful. If Ima was willing to go to these lengths, who knows what she might do if she realizes we've uncovered her secret."

A chill ran down Morty's spine. "You're right. We need a plan."

Suddenly, Willow gasped, her eyes flying open. "Someone's coming!"

Morty's jaw clenched, his eyes hardening with resolve. He straightened up, his portly frame radiating determination. "We can't let this stand," he declared, his voice low but fierce. "Ima Picky's reign of terror ends now."

Dr. Frankie Stein nodded, her stitched brow furrowing. "But Morty, we have to be careful. This could backfire spectacularly."

"I know the risks," Morty replied, running a hand through his wild, static-charged hair. "But think of all the people she's hurt. The businesses ruined, the lives upended. We owe it to Hollow Creek to set things right."

Willow Shadowmoon's ethereal voice cut through the tension. "The spirits are restless. They demand justice."

Morty paced the hidden room, his mind racing. "We need to gather all this evidence. Every photo, every letter, every scrap of paper that proves what Ima's been up to."

Dr. Frankie began sifting through the documents. "We should organize this systematically. Create a timeline of her sabotage."

"Good idea," Morty agreed. He paused, a wicked grin spreading across his face. "You could say we're about to serve Ima Picky her just desserts."

Willow groaned. "Really, Morty? Now?"

"Sorry," he chuckled. "Gallows humor. It's how I cope."

As they worked, Morty's thoughts churned. What would this mean for his restaurant? For his reputation? He pushed the doubts aside. Justice was more important than his personal concerns.

"We need to move quickly," Dr. Frankie said, glancing at her watch. "The longer we're here, the greater the chance of getting caught."

Morty nodded. "You're right. Let's get this wrapped up and head straight to the sheriff's office."

They worked feverishly, sorting and cataloging the damning evidence. Morty's hands trembled slightly as he handled each piece, the weight of their discovery settling on his shoulders.

"Do you think the authorities will believe us?" Willow asked, her voice barely above a whisper.

Morty paused, considering. "They'll have to. With all this evidence, it's impossible to ignore."

Dr. Frankie zipped up a bag full of documents. "We should make copies, just in case. I don't trust Ima not to have connections in high places."

"Smart thinking," Morty agreed. He glanced at his watch, feeling the pressure of time bearing down on them. "We need to wrap this up. Every minute we're here is another chance for Ima to catch on to what we're doing."

As they finished gathering the evidence, a sense of urgency filled the air. Morty's heart raced, adrenaline coursing through his veins. They were about to change everything in Hollow Creek, and there was no turning back now.

Morty hefted the bag of evidence, its weight a physical reminder of the gravity of their situation. He turned to his companions, determination etched on his face.

"Alright, team. Let's get out of here and—"

A sharp creak echoed through the house, cutting him off mid-sentence. Morty froze, his eyes darting to meet Dr. Frankie's and Willow's equally startled expressions.

"Did you hear that?" Willow whispered, her voice trembling.

Morty nodded, straining his ears. The house had fallen eerily silent again, but the tension in the air was palpable.

"Could be the wind," Dr. Frankie offered, but her tone lacked conviction.

Morty's grip tightened on the bag. "Let's not take any chances. We need to leave. Now."

They crept towards the door, each step deliberate and cautious. Morty's heart pounded in his chest, so loud he was certain the others could hear it. As they reached the threshold, another creak sounded, closer this time.

"Run," Morty hissed, abandoning all pretense of stealth.

They burst out of the room, thundering down the hallway. Morty's portly frame jiggled with each step, but adrenaline propelled him forward. Behind them, heavy footsteps echoed, gaining ground.

"The back door!" Dr. Frankie shouted, gesturing wildly.

They careened around a corner, nearly colliding with an end table. A vase toppled, shattering on the floor. Morty winced at the noise but didn't slow down.

As they neared the back door, a shadow fell across their path. Morty skidded to a halt, nearly losing his balance. There, blocking their escape, stood a figure shrouded in darkness.

"Going somewhere?" a familiar voice drawled, dripping with malice.

Best Served Dead

Morty's blood ran cold. He knew that voice. It was Ima Picky.

CHAPTER 12

Morty's eyes fluttered open. Darkness enveloped him, broken only by a sliver of light seeping under a door. His head throbbed. The coppery taste of blood lingered on his tongue.

"Mmph!" He tried to speak, but fabric muffled his words. Panic surged through him as realization dawned. Bound. Gagged. Trapped.

His heart raced, pounding against his ribs like a caged beast. Sweat beaded on his brow, trickling down his face. The wild salt-and-pepper hair that usually crackled with static now lay limp and damp against his forehead.

Morty strained against the ropes binding his wrists and ankles. They bit into his flesh, unyielding. He writhed, trying to loosen them, but succeeded only in tipping himself onto his side.

'Think, Morty, think!' he urged himself silently. 'What would you do if this were some ghoulish garnish?'

His culinary instincts kicked in. He began to catalogue his surroundings, much as he would ingredients for a new recipe. The room smelled musty, with undertones of mildew and... was that cinnamon?

'Focus!' he chided himself. 'This isn't the time for aromatic analysis.'

Morty's eyes, now adjusted to the gloom, darted around the room. Shadows loomed, transforming ordinary objects into monstrous shapes. A chair became a crouching gargoyle. A coat rack morphed into a skeletal spectre.

'If only I had my meat cleaver,' Morty mused. 'I'd dice these ropes faster than you can say "bone appetite"!'

He chuckled inwardly at his own pun, then sobered. This was no laughing matter. He needed to escape before his captor returned.

Morty rolled onto his stomach, ignoring the protest of his aching muscles. He inched forward, nose nearly touching the grimy floor. His portly frame made movement difficult, but determination fueled him.

'Come on, old boy,' he encouraged himself. 'You've navigated tighter spots in the walk-in freezer.'

As he crawled, Morty's chef's intuition catalogued potential tools. A loose floorboard? Too unwieldy. A rusty nail? Too fragile. He needed something sharp, sturdy, and within reach.

Suddenly, his nose caught a whiff of something familiar. Onions? Garlic? His culinary radar pinged. A kitchen must be nearby.

Hope surged through him. Where there was a kitchen, there were knives. And where there were knives, there was a chance at freedom.

Morty redoubled his efforts, squirming towards the source of the smell. His progress was slow, hampered by his bonds and his less-than-svelte physique.

'If I get out of this,' he vowed silently, 'I'm adding "escape artist workout" to my routine. Right after "perfecting plasma pumpkin pie".'

As he inched forward, a new sound reached his ears. Footsteps, growing louder. Someone was coming.

Morty froze, his heart hammering. He'd run out of time. The door creaked open, flooding the room with light.

A shadow fell across him. Morty looked up, blinking against the sudden brightness. His eyes widened in shock as he recognized the figure looming over him.

"Well, well," a familiar voice chuckled. "Looks like the chef is finally ready to spill the beans."

Morty's eyes darted around, desperate for an escape route. That's when he spotted it - a nearby table, laden with kitchen utensils. A glimmer of hope sparked in his chest.

'Bingo,' he thought. 'Now that's what I call a silver lining.'

With renewed determination, Morty began to inch his way towards the table. Every movement was calculated, his body tensed to minimize any sound. The ropes bit into his skin, but he gritted his teeth against the pain.

'Just a little further,' he urged himself. 'You can do this, Morty. Think of it as prepping for the world's most intense cooking competition.'

As he neared the table, his eyes locked onto a small paring knife perched precariously on the edge. It was perfect - sharp, manageable, and within reach.

Morty stretched his neck, positioning his mouth near the knife's handle. He could almost taste freedom.

'Here goes nothing,' he thought, opening his jaws wide.

With a swift motion, Morty clamped his teeth around the knife's handle. Success! He allowed himself a moment of triumph before focusing on the next step.

Carefully, he maneuvered the knife towards his bound wrists. The angle was awkward, and sweat beaded on his brow from the effort.

'Steady now,' he coached himself. 'This is just like carving the world's tiniest jack-o'-lantern.'

Morty began to saw at the ropes, his movements precise and controlled. He strained his ears for any sign of Peter's return, knowing that discovery now would spell disaster.

The rope began to fray, one strand at a time. Morty's heart raced with a mixture of fear and anticipation. He was so close to freedom, he could almost taste it - and it was sweeter than his famous phantom fudge.

With a final snap, the ropes fell away. Morty's wrists burned as blood rushed back into his hands. He quickly spat out the gag, sucking in deep breaths of musty air.

"Sweet pumpkin pie," he wheezed, massaging his jaw. "That was about as fun as eating ghost peppers blindfolded."

His heart hammered against his ribs as he assessed his surroundings. The room was dim, lit only by a single flickering bulb. Shadows danced on the walls, reminiscent of the spooky projections he used in his restaurant during Halloween.

'Focus, Morty,' he chided himself. 'This isn't the time for culinary comparisons.'

His eyes darted around, searching for an escape route. There, on the far side of the room - a partially open window. Hope bloomed in his chest like yeast in warm dough.

Morty pushed himself to his feet, his legs wobbling like overcooked spaghetti. He took a tentative step forward, wincing at the creak of the floorboard beneath his foot.

'Quiet as a mouse in a pantry,' he thought, carefully placing each step. 'Or Peter might serve you up as the main course.'

As he inched towards the window, Morty's mind raced. How had he ended up here? Who was the real killer? And most importantly, would he ever get to make his famous 'Graveyard Goulash' again?

The window drew closer with each careful step. Freedom was just a leap away, but one wrong move could turn this great escape into a recipe for disaster.

Just as Morty's fingers brushed the cool glass of the window, a sound froze him in place. Footsteps. Heavy and deliberate, they echoed from beyond the door.

'Bats and broomsticks!' Morty's mind screamed.

His eyes darted frantically around the room. A large, ornate cabinet loomed nearby. Without hesitation, Morty dove behind it, his portly frame barely squeezing into the tight space.

Heart pounding like a chef's knife on a cutting board, Morty held his breath. The footsteps grew louder, then paused just outside the door.

'Please don't come in,' Morty silently pleaded. 'I'm not ready to be the secret ingredient in someone else's stew.'

The doorknob rattled. Morty's fingers dug into the carpet, his wild hair standing even more on end. Time seemed to stretch like melted mozzarella.

After what felt like an eternity, the footsteps retreated. Morty let out a shaky breath, relief washing over him like a cool marinade.

"That was closer than a perfect soufflé," he muttered, easing out from behind the cabinet.

Morty glanced at the window, his ticket to freedom. With renewed determination, he shuffled towards it, his culinary-honed muscles tensing for the escape.

Morty grunted as he squeezed through the narrow window opening. His rotund belly proved a challenge, but years of kneading dough had given him surprising upper body strength.

"I'm like a sausage being stuffed into its casing," he whispered, wiggling free.

With a soft thud, Morty landed in a small courtyard. The cool night air kissed his face, a stark contrast to the stuffy room he'd just escaped. Tall walls loomed on all sides, their imposing presence making him feel like a garnish on an oversized plate.

His eyes darted around, searching for any sign of Peter or other threats. The courtyard was eerily quiet, save for the rustling of leaves in a gentle breeze.

"Now, where's the exit to this culinary catastrophe?" Morty muttered, his mind racing faster than a soufflé rising in a hot oven.

He spotted a rusty gate on the far side, but it was padlocked. A withered tree stood in one corner, its branches too flimsy to support his weight. Morty's heart sank like an undercooked cake.

"Think, Morty, think! You've gotten out of tighter spots than this... like that time with the possessed pumpkin pie."

As he scanned the walls again, a glimmer of hope caught his eye. A drainpipe ran up one side, disappearing over the top of the wall.

"Well, well," Morty chuckled softly. "Looks like I'll be climbing the beanstalk after all."

Morty approached the drainpipe, his portly frame casting a long shadow in the dim light. He grabbed it, testing its strength with a gentle tug.

"Don't fail me now, you glorified pasta noodle," he whispered.

With a deep breath, Morty began his ascent. His muscles strained, unused to this type of exertion. Sweat beaded on his brow as he inched upward.

"I should've... stuck to... lifting... saucepans," he panted between grunts.

Halfway up, the pipe creaked ominously. Morty froze, his heart pounding like a meat tenderizer.

"Easy does it," he coaxed himself. "Slow and steady wins the race... and doesn't plummet to an untimely demise."

Finally, his hands grasped the top of the wall. With a herculean effort, Morty hauled himself up, straddling the narrow ledge.

"I did it!" he wheezed, allowing himself a moment of triumph. "Take that, gravity!"

Catching his breath, Morty surveyed his surroundings. The unfamiliar landscape stretched out before him, a patchwork of shadows and faint lights.

"Now, where in the name of burnt toast am I?"

Morty's eyes darted from shadow to shadow as he crept along the narrow alleyway. His heart pounded like a sous chef frantically chopping onions.

"Easy now, Morty," he whispered to himself. "You're just a harmless, innocent chef out for a midnight stroll. Nothing suspicious here."

A cat yowled nearby, making him jump. He pressed himself against the cold brick wall, willing his bulky frame to melt into the darkness.

"Jumpy as a soufflé in an earthquake," Morty muttered, shaking his head.

He inched forward, his culinary-trained senses on high alert. The scent of garbage and damp concrete filled his nostrils.

"Not exactly the aroma I'd choose for my next signature dish," he quipped softly.

As he rounded a corner, voices drifted from a nearby street. Morty froze, holding his breath.

"...heard they're looking for that chef," a gruff voice said.

"Yeah, the one who cooks all that spooky food," another replied.

Morty's mind raced. "Spooky food? I prefer 'gastronomically haunting,' thank you very much."

He waited until the voices faded before moving on. The maze of alleys seemed endless, each turn leading to another shadowy passage.

"I feel like a noodle lost in my own lasagna," Morty grumbled.

Suddenly, a familiar sight caught his eye. The clock tower of the Hollow Creek Police Station loomed in the distance.

"Well, butter my biscuits," Morty exclaimed under his breath. "There's my ticket to freedom!"

He quickened his pace, hope surging through him like a perfectly timed soufflé rise.

"Hold on, innocence," Morty thought. "I'm coming to claim you, with a side of justice for dessert."

Morty burst through the police station doors, his wild salt-and-pepper hair crackling with static electricity and his once-pristine chef's whites now stained and tattered. The fluorescent lights buzzed overhead, casting a harsh glow on his disheveled appearance.

Officers and desk clerks turned to stare, their expressions a mix of shock and confusion. Morty's eyes darted around the room, taking in the scene like a chef surveying his kitchen before a busy dinner service.

"Well, hello there, officers!" Morty called out, his voice carrying a forced cheeriness that belied his frantic state. "I hope I'm not too late for the crime-solving soirée. I brought a dish to share – it's called 'Innocent Chef Surprise.'"

He approached the front desk, where a wide-eyed young officer sat frozen in place. Morty leaned in, his wild hair seeming to reach out towards the officer like tentacles.

"I don't suppose you have a comb handy?" Morty asked, patting his unruly mane. "No? Never mind, then. I'll just have to embrace the 'freshly electrocuted' look. It's all the rage in culinary circles, you know."

The officer blinked rapidly, finally finding his voice. "Sir, are you... are you Mortimer Graves?"

Morty's eyes lit up. "The one and only! Though I must say, I've had a few grave situations lately. Get it? Grave? Graves?" He chuckled at his own pun, then sobered quickly. "But in all seriousness, my good man, I've got a tale to tell that's spicier than my five-alarm ghost pepper goulash."

He leaned in closer, his voice dropping to a conspiratorial whisper. "And between you and me, that goulash once made the mayor hiccup fire for a week."

The young officer leaned back, overwhelmed by Morty's presence and the faint smell of rope fibers and sweat that clung to him. "Sir, you need to step back. You're a wanted man."

Morty's eyebrows shot up, disappearing into his wild hair. "Wanted? Oh, I'm flattered! But I'm afraid I'm already in a committed relationship with my kitchen. Though she can be a bit hot and cold, if you know what I mean."

He winked, then quickly sobered again. "But listen, my badge-wearing friend, I've been framed! Set up like a perfectly plated dessert, only this dish is anything but sweet."

CHAPTER 13

The October wind whistled through the pumpkin patch, rustling the dried cornstalks. Morty's wild hair danced in the breeze as he faced Peter, flanked by Dr. Frankie Stein and Willow Shadowmoon. Their eyes locked in a tense standoff.

Peter's Adam's apple bobbed nervously. "I-I don't know what you're talking about," he stammered, his voice barely above a whisper.

Morty's gaze hardened. "Cut the act, Peter. We know you did it."

Peter's face grew even paler, a sheen of sweat glistening on his forehead. "N-no, you've got it all wrong. I would never—"

"Enough!" Morty bellowed, his booming voice echoing across the patch. "Tell us the truth. Now."

Willow's violet eyes narrowed, her flowing robes billowing dramatically. "The spirits don't lie, Peter. They've shown us your deception."

Dr. Stein stepped forward, her piercing green eyes boring into Peter. "The evidence is clear. Confess, and perhaps we can help you."

Peter's shoulders slumped. He looked like a deflated balloon, all the fight drained out of him.

Morty's mind raced. How could this meek man be capable of such a heinous act? Yet the proof was undeniable.

"I... I..." Peter's voice cracked. Tears welled in his eyes.

Morty felt a pang of pity, quickly squashed by righteous anger. "Spit it out, man. We don't have all night."

As Peter opened his mouth to speak, a distant siren wailed. Red and blue lights flashed on the horizon.

Peter's knees buckled. He sank to the damp earth, crushing a small pumpkin beneath him. Orange pulp oozed between his fingers.

"I did it," he whispered, his voice trembling. "I poisoned Ima's squid ink pasta with pufferfish toxin."

Morty's stomach lurched. The confession hung in the air, heavy as the autumn mist.

Dr. Frankie Stein stepped forward, her tall frame casting a long shadow in the moonlight. "Why, Peter?" she demanded, her tone a mix of scientific curiosity and moral outrage. "What drove you to such extremes?"

Peter's head snapped up, his eyes wild. "You don't understand! None of you do!" he cried, his voice cracking. "Years of her cruel words, her constant belittling..."

Morty's fists clenched. He'd known Ima was harsh, but this...

"That doesn't justify murder," Willow interjected, her voice soft but firm.

Dr. Stein crouched beside Peter, her piercing gaze never leaving his face. "Explain yourself, Peter. We need to understand."

The distant sirens grew louder. Time was running out.

Peter's shoulders shook with silent sobs. "I just... I couldn't take it anymore. The humiliation, the constant fear..."

Morty's mind raced. How had he missed the signs? The quiet desperation in Peter's eyes, the way he flinched at Ima's approach...

Dr. Stein's voice cut through his thoughts. "Continue, Peter. We're listening."

Peter's voice grew stronger, a torrent of pent-up emotions breaking free. "Every day was torture. She'd mock my ideas, belittle my work, make me feel worthless."

A gust of wind sent dead leaves skittering across the pumpkin patch. Morty shivered, not from the cold.

"I became her punching bag," Peter continued, his eyes distant. "Nothing I did was ever good enough. She threatened to ruin my career if I left."

Morty's jaw clenched. He'd known Ima was harsh, but this level of cruelty...

"So you decided to kill her," Dr. Stein stated, her voice neutral.

Peter nodded, a tear sliding down his cheek. "I saw no other way out."

Morty's eyes narrowed. One piece of the puzzle remained. He stepped closer, looming over Peter.

"The pumpkin ice cream," Morty growled. "How did it fit into your plan?"

Peter flinched at Morty's tone. "I... I needed a distraction," he stammered.

"Explain," Morty demanded, his patience wearing thin.

Peter swallowed hard. "I knew your ice cream was famous. If suspicion fell on it..."

Morty's fists clenched. His family's legacy, used as a pawn in this twisted game.

"Keep talking," he growled, fighting to keep his anger in check.

Peter's shoulders slumped. "I snuck into your freezer after hours. Planted the tainted ice cream."

Morty's eyes widened. The audacity of it all.

"It was easy," Peter continued, his voice barely above a whisper. "No one questions Ima's assistant."

A chill ran down Morty's spine. He'd trusted Peter. They all had.

Peter's gaze darted between them. "I thought... if the ice cream was blamed, no one would look further."

Willow stepped forward, her violet eyes blazing. The air crackled with tension.

"You betrayed us all," she hissed, her voice low and dangerous.

Peter shrank back. Willow's presence seemed to fill the entire pumpkin patch.

"I... I didn't mean..." Peter stammered.

Willow cut him off. "Didn't mean what? To frame an innocent man? To destroy a family legacy?"

Her words hung in the air, sharp as knives. Peter looked away, unable to meet her gaze.

Morty watched, torn between anger and pity. The man before him was broken, desperate.

Willow's voice softened, but her eyes remained hard. "The spirits whisper of your pain, Peter. But they cannot condone your actions."

A sob escaped Peter's throat. The weight of his choices seemed to crush him.

Morty's mind raced. What now? Justice needed to be served, but how?

The wind picked up, whipping through the pumpkin vines. A storm was brewing, both in the sky and in their hearts.

Morty's brow furrowed, his wild hair dancing in the breeze. He needed a plan, fast.

"We can't let him slip away," Morty muttered, more to himself than the others.

Dr. Frankie Stein nodded, her piercing green eyes locked on Peter. "Indeed. This confession must be properly documented."

Morty's mind whirred like a possessed Kitchen-Aid. Then it hit him.

"My phone!" he exclaimed, fumbling in his apron pocket. "We'll record everything."

Dr. Stein's lips curled into a slight smile. "Excellent thinking, Mortimer."

Morty's stubby fingers trembled as he pulled out his phone. The orange case, decorated with tiny bats, seemed eerily appropriate.

"Peter," Morty said, his voice uncharacteristically serious. "We need you to repeat everything. For the record."

Peter's face paled further, if that was possible. He looked like a ghost among the pumpkins.

Dr. Stein stepped forward, her tall frame casting a long shadow in the fading light.

"Morty, Willow," she commanded, her voice calm yet authoritative. "Ensure Mr. Parasol doesn't leave. I'll contact Detective O'Lantern."

Morty nodded, his heart pounding. This was it. The moment of truth.

As Dr. Stein moved away, phone in hand, Morty couldn't help but wonder: Would this be enough to save the Halloween Festival?

Morty and Willow tightened their grip on Peter's trembling arms. Their eyes met over his hunched form, a silent pact forming between them. Justice for Ima, redemption for Hollow Creek.

The wind picked up, rustling through the pumpkin patch. Dried leaves skittered across their feet. Morty suppressed a shiver, unsure if it was from the chill or the gravity of the moment.

"You won't get away with this, Peter," Willow whispered, her violet eyes intense. "The spirits demand balance."

Peter whimpered, his thin frame sagging between them.

Meanwhile, Dr. Frankie Stein stepped away, her long fingers dancing across her phone's screen. The glow illuminated her striking features in the deepening twilight.

"Detective O'Lantern?" Her voice cut through the whisper of wind in the vines. "We have a situation at Hollow Creek Pumpkin Patch. Peter Parasol has confessed to Ima's murder."

Morty strained to hear the detective's response, but Dr. Stein's next words chilled him more than the autumn air.

"No, he's restrained for now, but we need immediate backup. The situation is... volatile."

Morty's mind raced. Volatile? What did she know that he didn't?

A distant rumble of thunder punctuated the tension. The storm was closing in, mirroring the tempest of emotions swirling through the pumpkin patch.

Dr. Frankie Stein ended the call with a decisive tap. Her green eyes locked onto Morty's, a mix of relief and steely determination in her gaze.

"They're on their way," she announced, her voice steady. "ETA ten minutes."

Morty's heart pounded against his ribs. Ten minutes. An eternity and an instant all at once.

"What do we do now?" he asked, his voice cracking slightly.

Dr. Stein's lips quirked in a humorless smile. "We wait, and we ensure our friend here doesn't get any ideas."

Peter sagged further, a broken sob escaping his lips.

Willow Shadowmoon stepped closer, her flowing hair seeming to catch nonexistent moonlight. When she spoke, her voice was soft yet resolute.

"Peter," she murmured, "the path ahead is dark, but not without hope. You must face the consequences of your actions."

Morty watched, fascinated, as Peter raised his tear-streaked face to meet Willow's gaze.

"How?" Peter croaked. "How can I possibly make amends for... for..."

"By accepting responsibility," Willow replied, her tone gentle but firm. "By seeking to understand the pain that drove you to this point, and vowing to transform it into something better."

A gust of wind swept through the pumpkin patch, carrying the scent of approaching rain. Morty shivered, wondering if the storm would break before help arrived.

Morty's eyes swept across the pumpkin patch, taking in the scene. The orange gourds glowed softly in the fading twilight, their carved faces seeming to watch the unfolding drama with eerie interest. A crisp autumn breeze rustled through the dry cornstalks, carrying with it the scent of fallen leaves and woodsmoke.

He took a deep breath, filling his lungs with the crisp air. The truth was out. Justice would be served. Hollow Creek could move forward.

"Well," Morty said, breaking the tense silence, "I suppose this gives new meaning to 'reaping what you sow,' eh Peter?"

Dr. Frankie Stein shot him a withering look. "Really, Morty? Puns? Now?"

Morty shrugged, a weak smile tugging at his lips. "What can I say? I'm just trying to 'squash' the tension."

Willow Shadowmoon stifled a groan, but Peter let out a strangled laugh that quickly turned into a sob.

As the sound of distant sirens grew louder, Morty's mind raced. The Halloween Festival was just days away. How would the town react to this news? Would they be able to salvage the celebration?

Suddenly, a flash of movement caught his eye. Something was darting between the pumpkins, heading straight for them.

"Look out!" Morty yelled, just as a blur of orange and black fur launched itself at Peter's face.

CHAPTER 14

The full moon hung low over Hollow Creek, casting long shadows across the deserted streets. Morty's footsteps crunched on fallen leaves as he and Willow made their way toward the pumpkin patch on the outskirts of town.

"You really think Peter's hiding out here?" Morty asked, his breath visible in the chilly night air.

Willow nodded, her violet eyes gleaming. "The spirits whisper of a troubled soul seeking refuge among the gourds."

Morty chuckled. "Well, if anyone can sniff out a suspect, it's you. Though I prefer using my nose for more delectable pursuits."

As they neared the patch, Morty noticed an odd glow emanating from within. It pulsed faintly, casting eerie shadows across the rows of pumpkins.

"You see that?" he whispered.

"Indeed," Willow murmured. "A most peculiar aura."

Morty's heart raced. They were close to solving this mystery, he could feel it. But a nagging doubt crept in. What if they were wrong about Peter?

"You sure about this, Willow? Peter always seemed so... harmless."

Willow's gaze hardened. "Appearances can be deceiving, my friend. Even the meekest soul may harbor darkness within."

Morty nodded grimly. She was right. They had to see this through.

Taking a deep breath, he stepped forward into the patch, the strange light washing over him.

Morty's shoes sank into the soft earth as he wove between the massive pumpkins. Their orange flesh gleamed in the mysterious light, creating grotesque shadows. His heart pounded, each beat echoing in his ears.

"Peter?" he called softly. "It's Morty. We just want to talk."

A rustling sound came from his left. Morty whirled, nearly losing his balance.

"Careful," Willow whispered behind him. "The vines are treacherous."

Morty nodded, steadying himself. He peered into the gloom, straining to see.

Suddenly, a figure burst from behind an enormous pumpkin. Peter Parasol stumbled forward, his eyes wide with terror. His usually neat clothes were disheveled, leaves and twigs caught in his thinning hair.

"S-stay back!" Peter cried, his voice cracking. "I... I didn't mean to..."

Morty raised his hands, trying to appear non-threatening. "Easy, Peter. We're not here to hurt you."

Peter's gaze darted between Morty and Willow, like a cornered animal seeking escape. Morty's mind raced. How had the meek assistant come to this?

"Peter," Morty said gently, "we know about Ima. We know what happened."

Peter's face crumpled. "You don't understand," he whimpered. "She... she was going to ruin everything."

Willow stepped forward, her violet eyes blazing with intensity. The crystals on her robes clinked softly as she moved. "Peter Parasol," she intoned, her voice steady and commanding, "you must confess to the murder of Ima Picky. The spirits demand justice."

Peter shrank back, his thin frame trembling. "N-no," he stammered, "you're wrong. I didn't... I couldn't..."

Morty watched the exchange, his mind whirring. He knew Peter was lying, but why? What could drive this timid man to murder?

"Come now, Peter," Morty said, injecting a note of levity into his voice. "Let's not sugar-coat this sour situation. The evidence is as clear as consommé."

Peter's eyes darted to Morty, confusion mixing with fear. "What... what evidence?"

Morty took a step closer, careful not to spook Peter further. "Well, for starters, there's the matter of your 'special' pasta sauce. A recipe to die for, wouldn't you say?"

Peter's face paled even further, if that was possible. "I don't know what you mean," he whispered.

"Oh, I think you do," Morty pressed on. "You see, I know a thing or two about exotic ingredients. And that sauce? It had a very particular flavor. One that masked something far more sinister."

Peter's resolve seemed to crumble before their eyes. His shoulders sagged, and he sank to his knees among the twisting vines. "She was going to fire me," he said, his voice barely audible. "After everything I'd done for her..."

Morty felt a pang of pity, despite everything. He glanced at Willow, seeing his own conflicted emotions mirrored in her eyes.

Morty reached into his pocket, his fingers closing around a small vial. He drew it out with a flourish, holding it up to catch the eerie glow of the pumpkin patch.

"Recognize this, Peter?" Morty asked, his voice uncharacteristically somber.

Peter's eyes widened, fixating on the dark liquid inside the vial. He swallowed hard, his Adam's apple bobbing visibly.

"Squid ink," Morty explained, turning the vial this way and that. "A culinary marvel, really. Rich in flavor, dramatic in presentation. But in your hands, it became something far more nefarious."

Willow stepped forward, her robes rustling in the cool night air. "You used it to mask the taste of the pufferfish toxin, didn't you?" she asked, her voice a mix of accusation and sadness.

Peter's silence was all the confirmation they needed.

Morty continued, his chef's mind piecing together the gruesome recipe. "The ink's intense flavor would have easily disguised the bitterness of the toxin. And its dark color? Perfect for hiding any telltale signs in the sauce."

A chilly breeze swept through the pumpkin patch, rustling the leaves and sending a shiver down Morty's spine. He couldn't help but admire the ingenuity, even as he recoiled at its purpose.

"It was... it was supposed to be perfect," Peter whispered, his voice barely audible over the wind. "She wasn't supposed to suffer."

Willow's eyes narrowed, gleaming with fierce determination in the dim light. She took a step closer to Peter, her violet gaze locked onto his trembling form.

"I see the truth within you, Peter," she intoned, her voice taking on an otherworldly quality. "Your mind cannot hide from me."

Willow raised her hands, adorned with jangling crystal bracelets, and pressed her fingertips to her temples. Her eyes rolled back, showing only whites.

"Years of torment," she murmured. "Endless criticism. Sleepless nights spent dreading another day under her thumb."

Peter whimpered, shrinking back against a massive pumpkin.

"You saw the pufferfish at the market," Willow continued, her voice growing stronger. "A spark of dark inspiration. The perfect revenge."

"Stop," Peter pleaded weakly. "Please..."

But Willow pressed on, relentless. "You imagined her praise, just once. Tasting your creation, declaring it perfection. Then silence. Forever."

Peter's legs gave out. He slumped to the ground, chest heaving with silent sobs.

"It's true," he choked out. "All of it. I... I killed Ima."

Morty's stomach clenched. He'd suspected, of course, but hearing the confession made it horribly real.

"I just wanted peace," Peter whispered, his voice raw with remorse. "But now I'll never have it."

Morty exhaled heavily, his breath visible in the chilly October air. He turned to Willow, their eyes meeting in the eerie glow of the pumpkin patch. A silent understanding passed between them.

"Well," Morty quipped, his voice tinged with dark humor, "I suppose that's one way to get out of a toxic work environment."

Willow's lips twitched, suppressing a smile. "Not the most advisable method, I'd say."

Peter remained crumpled on the ground, his sobs subsiding into quiet whimpers.

Morty stepped forward, fishing a pair of novelty handcuffs from his apron pocket. They were shaped like tiny skeletal hands. "Never thought I'd use these outside the kitchen," he muttered.

Just as he reached for Peter's wrist, a sudden wail pierced the night. Morty froze, his heart leaping into his throat.

Willow's eyes widened. "The authorities," she breathed.

The distant sound of sirens grew louder, red and blue lights beginning to dance at the edge of the pumpkin patch.

Morty's mind raced. They'd solved the case, but how would they explain their methods? Would anyone believe them?

"Well," he said, forcing a grin, "looks like our gourd times are about to get squashed."

The police cruisers screeched to a halt at the edge of the pumpkin patch, their headlights casting long shadows across the field. Morty and Willow exchanged a quick glance before stepping back, allowing the officers to rush in.

"Hands where we can see them!" shouted the lead officer, his flashlight beam cutting through the darkness.

Morty raised his hands, still clutching the skeletal handcuffs. "Officers, we can explain," he said, his voice steady despite the adrenaline coursing through him.

As the police surrounded Peter, Morty felt a strange mix of relief and exhaustion wash over him. He watched as they gently lifted the sobbing man to his feet, reciting his rights.

Willow leaned close, her voice barely above a whisper. "It's over, Morty. We did it."

Morty nodded, his eyes never leaving Peter as the officers led him towards the waiting patrol car. A lump formed in his throat as he realized the full weight of what had transpired.

"My name," he thought, his chest tightening. "It's finally cleared."

The crisp autumn air carried the scent of decay and new beginnings. As Peter disappeared into the back of the police cruiser, Morty couldn't help but feel a bittersweet pang of sympathy for the man.

"Sometimes," he mused aloud, "the scariest monsters are the ones we create ourselves."

Willow touched his arm gently. "Come on, Morty. They'll want our statements."

With a deep breath, Morty squared his shoulders and followed Willow towards the flashing lights, leaving behind the shadowy pumpkin patch and the ghosts of accusations that had haunted him for so long.

As the last police car pulled away, its red and blue lights fading into the distance, Morty and Willow found themselves alone in the pumpkin patch. The moon hung low in the sky, casting an eerie glow over the field of orange globes.

Morty plopped down on a nearby hay bale, his chef's hat askew. "Well, that was quite the recipe for disaster," he quipped, his voice tinged with exhaustion.

Willow settled beside him, her violet eyes reflecting the moonlight. "Indeed. Though I must say, your culinary clue-finding skills were quite... appetizing."

A chuckle escaped Morty's lips. "And your psychic prowess was truly out of this world, my dear."

They sat in comfortable silence for a moment, the cool night air rustling through the dried cornstalks nearby. Morty could smell the earthy scent of pumpkins mingling with the faint aroma of wood smoke from distant bonfires.

"You know," Willow mused, "I never thought I'd say this, but I'm glad we teamed up, Morty. Your practical approach balanced my... shall we say, more ethereal methods."

Morty grinned, his eyes twinkling. "We do make quite the pair, don't we? Like candy corn and caramel apples."

As they shared a laugh, a sudden gust of wind swept through the patch, sending a flurry of leaves dancing around them. Morty shivered, not entirely from the cold.

"Say, Willow," he began, his tone turning serious. "Do you think-"

But before he could finish, a blood-curdling scream pierced the night, echoing from the direction of Hollow Creek's haunted hayride.

CHAPTER 15

The Ghoulish Gourmet's kitchen gleamed under the flickering orange lights, a cauldron of pumpkin soup bubbling ominously on the stove. Morty wiped his brow, smearing a streak of orange across his forehead. He glanced at the clock – 11:30 PM. Almost the witching hour.

"Ladies, gather 'round," Morty called, gesturing to Dr. Frankie Stein and Willow Shadowmoon. "It's time we put our heads together and solve this ghastly affair."

Dr. Stein glided over, her lab coat swishing. "I hope you have something substantial, Morty. The festival starts tomorrow, and we're running out of time."

Willow floated to join them, crystals tinkling softly around her neck. "The spirits are restless. We must act swiftly."

Morty nodded, his wild hair bobbing. "Indeed we must. I've been cooking up more than just culinary delights, my friends. I believe I've found our killer."

Dr. Stein's eyebrow arched. "Do tell."

Morty reached under the counter and pulled out a file folder. "It's Peter Parasol. And I've got the evidence to prove it."

Willow gasped, her violet eyes widening. "The tourism board director? But why?"

Morty spread the contents of the folder across the stainless steel prep table. Newspaper clippings, financial reports, and photographs littered the surface.

"It's all about money and power," Morty explained, tapping a finger on a financial statement. "Peter's been embezzling funds from the tourism board for years. He was using the Halloween Festival as a cover."

Dr. Stein leaned in, her piercing green eyes scanning the documents. "Clever. The influx of tourists would mask any discrepancies in the books."

Morty nodded. "Exactly. But Ima Picky was onto him. She threatened to expose his scheme unless he gave her a bigger cut of the profits."

Willow's brow furrowed. "So he silenced her permanently."

"With this," Morty said, producing a small vial filled with white powder. "Pufferfish toxin. I found traces of it in the remnants of Ima's last meal – my squid ink pasta."

Dr. Stein's eyes narrowed. "Tetrodotoxin. Highly potent and difficult to detect. Where did you get this sample?"

Morty grinned, a mischievous twinkle in his eye. "Let's just say I have connections in the culinary underworld. It pays to know your poisonous ingredients in my line of work."

Willow shuddered. "How dreadful. To think he used your own creation as a murder weapon, Morty."

Morty's face darkened. "Indeed. It's an insult to the culinary arts. And to think, he nearly got away with pinning it on me."

Dr. Stein nodded solemnly. "The evidence is compelling. But how do we prove it to the authorities?"

Morty's eyes gleamed with determination. "I have a plan. But it's going to take all of us working together."

Outside, a gust of wind rattled the restaurant's windows, sending autumn leaves skittering across the darkened street. Jack-o'-lanterns grinned from nearby porches, their flickering flames casting eerie shadows.

Willow shivered. "The veil between worlds grows thin. We must act quickly before the spirits of Hollow Creek lose faith in us."

Dr. Stein rolled her eyes. "Let's focus on the tangible evidence, shall we? Morty, what exactly did you have in mind?"

Morty leaned in close, lowering his voice. "We need to catch Peter red-handed. Force a confession out of him."

Dr. Stein frowned. "That's easier said than done. He's been careful so far."

Morty's eyes twinkled. "Ah, but we have something he doesn't expect – the element of surprise. And a secret weapon."

Willow tilted her head. "What secret weapon?"

Morty grinned, spreading his arms wide. "Me, of course! Who would suspect a bumbling chef of being an amateur detective?"

Dr. Stein chuckled. "You're many things, Morty, but bumbling isn't one of them. Still, it could work to our advantage."

Willow nodded eagerly. "Yes, and I can use my crystals to channel positive energy and cloud his judgment!"

Dr. Stein sighed. "Let's stick to methods that will hold up in court, shall we? Morty, what's the next step?"

Morty rubbed his hands together gleefully. "We need to lure Peter out into the open. Somewhere he feels safe, but where we can control the situation."

A sudden crash from the alley behind the restaurant made them all jump. Morty's hand instinctively reached for a nearby cleaver.

"What was that?" Willow whispered, her eyes wide with fear.

Dr. Stein moved swiftly to the back door, peering out into the darkness. "Probably just a cat knocking over a trash can. But we should be more careful. Peter might have allies watching us."

Morty nodded grimly. "All the more reason to act quickly. We need to set our trap before the festival begins tomorrow."

Willow wrung her hands nervously. "But how? Where?"

Morty's eyes lit up. "I have an idea. But it's going to require some... unconventional ingredients."

Dr. Stein raised an eyebrow. "Why do I have a feeling I'm not going to like this?"

Morty grinned, a manic gleam in his eye. "Trust me, it'll be a piece of cake. Or rather, a very large, very unusual cake."

As Morty began to outline his plan, the wind outside grew stronger, howling through the empty streets of Hollow Creek. In the distance, a clock tower began to chime midnight. The witching hour had begun, and with it, the final countdown to expose a killer and save Halloween.

Morty stood before a massive, grotesque cake sculpture that vaguely resembled a human form. Its bulbous body was covered in sickly green fondant, with protruding candy eyeballs and licorice veins.

"Well, what do you think?" Morty asked, grinning proudly.

Dr. Stein circled the monstrosity, her brow furrowed. "It's... certainly unsettling. But how exactly will this help us catch Peter?"

Morty patted the cake's lumpy side. "Simple. I'll be inside it."

Willow gasped. "You're going to hide inside that thing?"

"Precisely," Morty nodded. "Peter won't suspect a thing. I'll wheel myself into the pumpkin patch and keep watch."

Dr. Stein looked skeptical. "And if he sees you?"

Morty's eyes twinkled mischievously. "Then I'll offer him a slice."

As they discussed the finer points of the plan, a chilly October breeze rattled the restaurant's windows. Outside, jack-o'-lanterns flickered ominously in the darkness. Morty felt a mix of excitement and trepidation churning in his stomach.

"It's risky," Willow said softly, touching Morty's arm. "Are you sure about this?"

Morty covered her hand with his, his resolve strengthening. "I have to try. For the festival. For Hollow Creek. For all of us."

With a deep breath, Morty began to climb into the cake sculpture. As the others helped seal him inside, he couldn't shake the feeling that everything was about to change.

Dr. Stein approached the grotesque cake, her green eyes glinting in the dim light. She held out a small, flesh-colored device.

"Here," she said, her voice low and serious. "This will keep us connected."

Morty's hand emerged from a gap in the fondant, grasping the earpiece. "Ah, my very own cake comm. How deliciously clandestine!"

Willow hovered nearby, her violet eyes wide with concern. "Be careful, Morty. The veil between worlds feels... thin tonight."

"Don't worry, my dear," Morty chuckled, his voice muffled by layers of cake. "I'm more scared of going stale than any spectral shenanigans."

As Morty prepared to roll out, Dr. Stein's hand rested on the cake's surface. "Remember, blend in. Use your culinary creativity if anyone gets suspicious."

With a deep breath, Morty began his journey. The cake creaked ominously as it moved, leaving a trail of crumbs behind.

Outside, the pumpkin patch loomed. Morty's heart raced as he maneuvered between jack-o'-lanterns and corn stalks. The earpiece crackled.

"Any sign of Peter?" Willow's anxious voice came through.

"Negative," Morty whispered. "But I spy some under-decorated gourds. Truly frightening."

He inched forward, the smell of damp earth and rotting pumpkins filling his nostrils. A nearby scarecrow seemed to watch him, its button eyes gleaming in the moonlight.

Morty's culinary instincts kicked in. He began arranging fallen leaves and vines around his cake base, blending into the festive scenery.

Suddenly, footsteps crunched nearby. Morty froze, his pulse pounding. Was it Peter? Or just an innocent pumpkin picker?

The cake stood motionless, a monstrous confection among the harvest decorations, waiting.

The footsteps grew closer. Morty held his breath, sweat beading on his brow beneath the layers of fondant and frosting. A shadow fell across his cake disguise.

"What in the name of All Hallows' Eve?" A familiar voice muttered.

Morty's heart leapt. It was Peter Parasol.

Seizing the moment, Morty burst from his sugary cocoon. "Surprise, Peter! Your gourd-geous reign of terror ends now!"

Peter stumbled backward, his face a mask of shock. "Morty? What are you—"

"Save the half-baked excuses," Morty interrupted, brushing cake crumbs from his apron. "We know you're the killer, Peter. Your recipe for revenge has gone sour."

Peter's eyes darted left and right, searching for an escape route. "You're mad, Morty. Too many fumes from that kitchen of yours."

Morty tapped his earpiece. "Dr. Stein, Willow, I've found our pumpkin-headed perpetrator."

"We're on our way," Dr. Stein's cool voice replied.

Peter lunged forward, attempting to knock Morty aside. But the chef's bulk, still padded with cake, held firm.

"Not so fast, you culinary criminal," Morty grunted, grabbing Peter's arm. "I may be a sweet treat, but I'm no pushover."

The two men grappled among the pumpkins, orange gourds rolling in all directions. Morty's mind raced. He had to keep Peter here until the others arrived.

"Tell me, Peter," Morty panted, "was it worth it? Poisoning poor Ima over a bad review?"

Peter's face contorted with rage. "She ruined me! My restaurant was everything!"

Morty's eyes widened. Was Peter about to confess?

"Years of abuse," Peter spat, his eyes wild. "Every dish I created, she tore apart. My dreams, my passion—all crushed under her vicious pen!"

Morty maintained his grip on Peter's arm, feeling the man tremble. "So you decided to serve her a final, fatal dish?"

Peter's shoulders slumped. The fight drained from him like overcooked pasta losing its bite. "I... I just wanted her to stop. To feel what it was like to have something you love turn against you."

A rustle in the nearby corn stalks announced Willow's arrival. Her violet eyes glowed in the moonlight as she emerged, a small crystal dangling from her hand.

"The spirits guided us, Morty," Willow intoned. "Now, let's ensure this confession sticks like burnt caramel."

Morty nodded, a plan forming. "Peter, you know my reputation for culinary magic. Care to taste a morsel of truth?"

He produced a small, elaborately decorated cupcake from his pocket. Peter eyed it warily.

"What is that?" he asked, voice quavering.

"Just a little recipe passed down through generations of Graves," Morty replied, his tone casual. "Said to reveal one's deepest secrets. Care for a bite?"

Peter's eyes darted between Morty and the cupcake. Willow began a low, ethereal chant, her crystal swaying hypnotically.

"I... I..." Peter stammered, then crumbled. "Fine! I did it! I poisoned Ima's pasta with pufferfish toxin. I couldn't take it anymore!"

As Peter's confession poured out, Willow's crystal glowed brightly. Unbeknownst to Peter, it was capturing every word on video.

A sudden crunch of leaves broke the tense atmosphere. Detective Jack O'Lantern stumbled into view, his tie askew and a half-eaten doughnut clutched in one hand.

"Ah-ha!" he exclaimed, spraying crumbs. "I knew if I followed the smell of Morty's cupcakes, I'd crack this case wide open!"

Morty raised an eyebrow. "Detective, how long have you been lurking in those bushes?"

"Long enough to hear this pumpernickel confess!" Jack declared, pointing dramatically at Peter with his doughnut.

Peter's face crumpled. "It's Parasol, actually," he mumbled.

Jack waved his hand dismissively. "Potato, tomato. You're under arrest, Mr. Parsnip!"

The detective fumbled for his handcuffs, nearly dropping them twice before securing them around Peter's wrists. Jack puffed out his chest, clearly proud of himself.

"You have the right to remain silent," he began, then frowned. "Or was it the right to party? No, that's not right..."

Morty sighed, pinching the bridge of his nose. "Perhaps you should focus on getting him to the station, Detective."

As Jack led Peter away, Morty couldn't help but feel a twinge of pity for the meek man. He turned to Willow, who was tucking away her crystal.

"Well," Morty said, "I suppose that wraps up our little Halloween whodunit."

The autumn wind whistled through the pumpkin patch as Morty, Dr. Frankie Stein, Willow Shadowmoon, and Detective Jack O'Lantern made their way back to The Ghoulish Gourmet. Leaves crunched underfoot, their vibrant oranges and reds a stark contrast to the somber mood.

As they approached the restaurant, a sea of expectant faces greeted them. The townspeople, their features illuminated by flickering jack-o'-lanterns, waited with bated breath.

Morty's heart swelled. He cleared his throat. "My friends," he began, his voice cracking slightly, "the mystery is solved. Peter Parasol has been arrested for the murder of Ima Picky."

A collective gasp rippled through the crowd. Willow placed a reassuring hand on Morty's shoulder.

"But how?" someone called out. "Why?"

Morty sighed. "It seems our dear Peter had a beef with Ima's culinary critiques. He thought poisoning her squid ink pasta would be the perfect revenge."

Detective Jack chimed in, "Yeah, he really noodled that one!"

The crowd groaned at Jack's attempt at humor. Dr. Frankie Stein rolled her eyes.

"The important thing," Morty continued, "is that our Halloween Festival can proceed without fear. And it's all thanks to the support of this wonderful community."

Cheers erupted from the gathering. Morty felt a lump form in his throat. He hadn't expected such an outpouring of emotion.

"I promise," he said, his voice thick with feeling, "to keep serving up the spookiest, most delectable dishes this side of the cemetery. The Ghoulish Gourmet isn't just a restaurant; it's a home for all of us odd ducks."

As the crowd applauded, Morty caught Willow's eye. She smiled enigmatically, her violet eyes twinkling in the moonlight. For a moment, he felt as if he could face any challenge, as long as he had his friends by his side.

The crowd dispersed, leaving Morty and Willow alone in The Ghoulish Gourmet. Morty's wild hair seemed to droop with exhaustion.

"What a day," he sighed, collapsing into a chair shaped like a tombstone.

Willow glided to the kitchen. "I sense we both need sustenance."

Morty chuckled. "You don't need psychic powers to figure that out."

The clock struck midnight as Willow returned, carrying two steaming plates. Morty's eyes widened.

"Is that my Mummy Meatloaf?"

"With extra bandages," Willow winked.

Outside, a chilly October wind rustled through the trees, sending a flurry of orange and red leaves dancing past the window. Jack-o'-lanterns flickered on nearby porches, casting eerie shadows.

Morty took a bite and groaned with pleasure. "I'd forgotten how good this tastes when I'm not the one cooking it."

Willow smiled, her ethereal presence softened by the warm candlelight. "The spirits whispered your recipe to me."

"Did they now?" Morty raised an eyebrow. "Or did you peek at my secret cookbook?"

Willow's laughter tinkled like wind chimes. "A true mystic never reveals her sources."

As they ate, Morty felt a warmth spreading through him that had nothing to do with the food. He looked at Willow, her long dark hair shimmering in the candlelight.

"You know," he said softly, "I couldn't have solved this without you."

Willow's violet eyes met his. "We make quite the team, don't we? The chef and the seer."

Suddenly, a loud crash echoed from the kitchen. Morty jumped to his feet, nearly knocking over the table.

"What in the name of all that's spooky was that?"

CHAPTER 16

The jack-o'-lantern candles flickered, casting dancing shadows across the Ghoulish Gourmet's freshly painted walls. Morty sank into his chair, inhaling the scent of pumpkin spice and brimstone. His hair crackled with static as he ran a hand through it.

"Who would've thought?" he mused aloud. "From a murder to reopening in just a month."

Morty's mind drifted to the whirlwind of events - the mysterious poisonings, the late-night sleuthing, the unlikely alliances forged. He chuckled, remembering how he'd nearly set the kitchen ablaze testing his "Flambéed Phantoms" recipe.

A crisp autumn breeze rustled the fake cobwebs adorning the windows. Outside, golden leaves skittered across the sidewalk. Morty's chest swelled with emotion.

"I couldn't have done it alone," he whispered, raising an invisible toast.

The creak of the front door jolted him from his reverie. Morty's eyes widened as he spotted his first customers - a young couple, their cheeks flushed from the chilly air.

"Welcome to the Ghoulish Gourmet!" he boomed, leaping to his feet. His apron, adorned with grinning skulls, fluttered as he rushed to greet them. "I hope you brought your appetite for the extraordinary!"

The woman giggled nervously. "We heard about your, um, unique menu."

Morty's eyes twinkled mischievously. "Oh, you're in for a treat! Or maybe a trick. Sometimes it's hard to tell the difference around here."

He ushered them to a cozy booth, handing them menus shaped like tombstones. "May I recommend our bone-chilling butternut squash soup?"

As Morty turned back towards the kitchen, a sudden gust of wind swept through the restaurant. The door swung open, and there stood Willow, glowing with excitement. Morty's heart skipped a beat.

"Willow!" he exclaimed, his voice cracking slightly. "You're just in time!"

Willow glided in, her flowing robes rustling. "The spirits led me here, Morty. They whispered of culinary delights beyond mortal imagination."

Morty grinned, warmth spreading through his chest. "Well, who am I to argue with the spirits? Come, let me show you the kitchen."

As they walked, Willow's gaze darted around the room. "The veil between worlds is thin here. Your decorations... they speak to the otherworldly."

"You like them?" Morty asked, gesturing to a particularly gruesome fake spider. "I call him Herbert."

Willow laughed, a sound like tinkling bells. "Herbert suits him."

In the kitchen, Morty grabbed two aprons. "Care to help me whip up some supernatural sustenance?"

Willow's eyes sparkled. "I thought you'd never ask."

Side by side, they began to work. Morty couldn't help but notice how naturally they moved together, like a well-choreographed dance.

"Pass me the eye of newt, would you?" Morty quipped, reaching for a jar of olives.

Willow smirked. "Careful, Morty. In the wrong hands, that could be a powerful ingredient indeed."

As the sun dipped below the horizon, Hollow Creek transformed. Jack-o'-lanterns flickered to life, casting eerie shadows across the cobblestone streets. Costumed revelers emerged from their homes, a parade of monsters, ghouls, and fantastical creatures.

Morty adjusted his chef's hat, now adorned with plastic spiders. "Shall we join the madness, my dear?"

Willow's eyes glimmered. "I thought you'd never ask."

They stepped out into the crisp autumn air. Fallen leaves crunched beneath their feet. The town square buzzed with excitement, a cauldron of laughter and chatter.

"Look at that!" Morty pointed to a towering haunted house. "Bet it's not as scary as my kitchen on a busy night."

Willow squeezed his hand. "I don't know, Morty. I've seen your kitchen. It's formidable."

They weaved through the crowd. A child in a werewolf costume howled as they passed.

"Impressive lungs on that one," Morty chuckled.

Willow nodded sagely. "The wolf spirit is strong in him."

They approached the pumpkin carving contest. Intricate designs adorned the orange gourds.

Morty whistled. "Now that's art. Almost makes me want to retire from cooking and take up gourd sculpting."

"Don't you dare," Willow said, her tone mock-serious. "The culinary world needs you, Mortimer Graves."

As they admired the pumpkins, a scream pierced the air. Not one of joy or excitement, but genuine terror.

Morty and Willow exchanged a look. "That," Morty said, "didn't sound like part of the festivities."

The scream had come from the direction of The Ghoulish Gourmet. Morty's heart raced. He and Willow rushed towards the restaurant, pushing through the costumed crowd.

As they approached, a waft of pungent aromas hit them. Morty's nostrils flared. "That's my Vampire's Delight soup! And... oh no, the Witch's Brew stew!"

They burst through the doors. The restaurant was packed, every table filled with eager diners. But something was off.

"Great googly moogly," Morty gasped.

His signature dishes were moving. The soup bubbled and hissed, tendrils of steam reaching out like grasping fingers. The stew in each bowl swirled of its own accord, creating miniature whirlpools.

A woman in a cat costume shrieked as her spoonful of soup tried to crawl back into the bowl.

Morty's mind raced. *What in the name of Julia Child's whisk is happening?*

"Morty," Willow whispered, "did you... enchant the food?"

He shook his head vigorously. "No! Well, not intentionally."

A man at the counter called out, "Hey, chef! Is this part of the Halloween gimmick?"

Morty forced a smile. "Of course! Nothing says spooky quite like, uh, sentient soup!"

Inside, he was panicking. *How do I fix this without ruining the festival?*

Willow's eyes gleamed with sudden inspiration. "I have an idea," she murmured to Morty. "Follow my lead."

She glided to the center of the restaurant, her flowing robes swishing dramatically. "Ladies and gentlemen," she announced in her soft yet commanding voice, "you are witnessing a rare celestial event!"

Morty watched, bewildered, as Willow raised her arms theatrically. The crystals adorning her sleeves caught the light, casting eerie reflections across the walls.

"The veil between worlds has thinned," she continued, "allowing spirits to inhabit these delectable dishes!"

The diners gasped in awe. Morty felt a surge of admiration for Willow's quick thinking.

"But fear not," Willow proclaimed, "for I shall guide these wayward spirits back to their realm."

She began to chant in a language Morty didn't recognize. To his amazement, the food gradually settled.

"Now," Willow said with a flourish, "you may enjoy your meals in peace."

The restaurant erupted in applause. Morty exhaled in relief.

"That was brilliant," he whispered to Willow. "How did you do that?"

She winked. "A good psychic never reveals her secrets. Now, shall we continue our evening?"

As they slipped out, Morty couldn't shake the feeling that there was more to this mystery than met the eye.

The town square clock chimed midnight, its deep resonance echoing through the now-quiet streets of Hollow Creek. Morty watched as the last of the festival-goers drifted away, their laughter fading into the crisp autumn air.

"Another Halloween for the books," he mused.

Willow nodded, her eyes reflecting the flickering street lamps. "The veil remains thin tonight. Can you feel it, Morty?"

He shivered, unsure if it was from the chill or Willow's words. "I feel... something."

They walked hand-in-hand towards The Ghoulish Gourmet, crunching through fallen leaves. Jack-o'-lanterns still grinned from porches, their candles guttering low.

"Your zombie fingers were a hit," Willow said, squeezing his hand.

Morty chuckled. "And your crystal ball readings had them spellbound."

They reached the restaurant, its windows dark. Morty fumbled with his keys, a sudden weariness washing over him.

"Ready for our next adventure?" Willow asked softly as the lock clicked open.

Morty paused, one foot over the threshold. "With you? Always."

They stepped inside, the door closing behind them with a gentle thud. The future, like the night, was full of delicious possibilities.

As they entered The Ghoulish Gourmet, Morty flicked on the lights. The restaurant's macabre decor cast eerie shadows across the room.

"Home sweet haunted home," Morty quipped, his eyes twinkling.

Willow laughed, a sound like tinkling bells. "It's perfect."

They made their way to the kitchen, Morty's sanctuary. The polished stainles steel gleamed under the fluorescent lights.

"Nightcap?" Morty asked, reaching for a bottle of blood-red wine.

"You read my mind," Willow replied, perching on a nearby stool.

As Morty poured, a sudden crash echoed from the dining room. They froze.

"Did you hear that?" Willow whispered, her eyes wide.

Morty's heart raced. "Maybe it's just the wind?"

Another crash, louder this time. Definitely not the wind.

"Stay here," Morty said, grabbing a rolling pin.

He crept towards the dining room, adrenaline pumping. The door creaked as he pushed it open.

A shadowy figure stood among overturned chairs. It turned, eyes glinting in the darkness.

Morty's grip tightened on the rolling pin. "Who's there?"

The figure lunged forward. Morty stumbled back, his heart pounding.

"Willow, call Detective O'Lantern!" he shouted.

The intruder rushed past him, knocking him off balance. By the time Morty regained his footing, the mysterious figure had vanished into the night.

Left behind was a crumpled note. Morty's hands shook as he unfolded it.

"Your recipes are mine, Graves. This is just the appetizer."

Morty swallowed hard. What had started as a perfect evening had suddenly become a recipe for disaster.

Morty paced back and forth in the kitchen, his mind racing. The intruder had disappeared into the night, leaving behind a note that sent chills down Morty's spine.

"What does it say?" Willow asked, her voice trembling.

Morty handed her the note. "It says that my recipes are theirs and this is just the beginning."

Willow's eyes widened in fear. "Who could want your recipes?"

Morty shook his head, unable to come up with an answer. "I don't know, but we need to find out before they come back."

He reached for the phone to call Detective O'Lantern, but it was dead. Morty cursed under his breath.

"Did they cut our phone line?" Willow asked, her voice rising in panic.

Morty nodded grimly. "And probably our power too."

He grabbed a flashlight and handed one to Willow. "We need to check the circuit breaker outside."

They cautiously made their way through the dark restaurant and stepped outside. As expected, the power was out and someone had tampered with the wires.

"We have to fix this," Morty said determinedly.

They worked together to repair the wires and soon enough the power was restored. But when they went back inside, they found that their computer had been hacked and all of their recipe files were gone.

"This can't be happening," Willow whispered in shock.

Morty's heart sank as he stared at his empty computer screen. Their hard work and secret recipes were now in someone else's hands.

"We need to call Detective O'Lantern," Morty said with a sense of urgency.

But when he tried calling again, there was still no dial tone. The intruder must have cut their phone line once more.

"We have to go to his office," Willow suggested, clutching onto Morty's arm.

He nodded in agreement and they quickly locked up the restaurant and drove to the police station. Detective O'Lantern listened to their story with a grave expression.

"I had a feeling something like this would happen," he said, shaking his head. "There have been reports of stolen recipes from other restaurants in the area as well."

Morty's heart sank even further. He couldn't believe that someone would want to steal his recipes and ruin his business.

"What do we do now?" Willow asked, her voice trembling.

"I'll launch an investigation and see if I can track down the culprit," Detective O'Lantern replied, taking notes on their statement. "But in the meantime, I suggest you both be careful. This person seems determined to get their hands on your recipes."

Morty and Willow thanked him before leaving the station. They returned to the restaurant, both lost in thought.

"We need to figure out who could have done this," Morty said finally, breaking the silence.

Willow nodded in agreement. They spent hours going through past employees, competitors, and even regular customers who always seemed too interested in their recipes. But nothing seemed to lead them closer to finding the culprit.

"Maybe it's someone we wouldn't suspect," Willow suggested after exhausting all possibilities.

Morty sighed and rubbed his temples. "I don't know anymore."

Just then, there was a knock on the door. Morty's heart skipped a beat as he cautiously approached it and peered through the peephole. It was just a delivery man holding a small package.

"Who is it?" Willow asked nervously as Morty opened the door.

"Just a delivery man," he replied, relieved but still wary.

The man handed him the package and left without saying a word. Morty opened it carefully and found a flash drive inside with a note.

"Play me."

Morty and Willow stared at the flash drive with confusion. Who could have sent it?

"Should we play it?" Willow asked, biting her lip.

Morty hesitated, but his curiosity got the best of him. He inserted the flash drive into his computer and a video file popped up.

It was a video of their restaurant kitchen, but at night when they were closed. Morty recognized the date in the corner - it was from last week when they had stayed late to finish some paperwork.

The camera zoomed in on their computer, showing someone typing on it. Morty's heart raced as he recognized his recipes being downloaded onto a USB drive.

"That's...that's our restaurant," Willow said with disbelief.

The video continued for a few more minutes before ending abruptly. Morty turned to Willow with determination in his eyes.

"We need to find out who has been spying on us," he said firmly.

Morty picked up his phone, his fingers trembling slightly as he dialed Detective O'Lantern's number. "Detective? It's Morty. We've got something you need to see."

An hour later, Detective O'Lantern sat in Morty's office, his eyes fixed on the security footage playing on the computer screen. "Well, I'll be damned," he muttered, leaning back in his chair.

Willow, standing behind them, couldn't contain her excitement. "So, what do you think? Is this enough evidence?"

The detective nodded slowly. "It's a start. Let me do some digging." He stood up, straightening his coat. "I'll be in touch soon."

Days passed, filled with anxious waiting. Finally, Detective O'Lantern called them back to his office.

"You're not going to believe this," he began, a hint of triumph in his voice. "Remember Jake, your former sous chef?"

Morty's eyes widened. "Jake? But he left months ago to work at that new place across town."

"Exactly," O'Lantern continued. "Turns out, he's been busy. We've linked him to a string of recipe thefts across several restaurants in the area. Your video was the missing piece we needed."

Willow gasped. "So it was Jake all along? But why?"

The detective's expression turned grim. "Money. He's been selling these recipes online to the highest bidder. But don't worry, we've got him now. Your recipes are safe. And we now have justice for Ima."

Relief washed over Morty and Willow. As they left the police station, Morty turned to Willow. "I can't believe we didn't see it coming. We need to be more careful from now on."

Willow nodded, squeezing his hand. "We will be. But let's focus on the positive. Our restaurant is still thriving, and now we have a story to tell."

In the weeks that followed, news of solving the murder and recipe theft spread, drawing curious diners from all over. Detective O'Lantern became a regular, always seated at his favorite corner table.

One evening, as Morty surveyed his packed restaurant, a smile spread across his face. He caught Willow's eye across the room, and they shared a moment of silent understanding. They had weathered the storm and come out stronger.

"You know," Morty said later that night as they closed up, "I've been thinking. Maybe it's time we expand. Open a second location in the next town over."

Willow's eyes lit up. "Really? You think we're ready?"

Morty nodded confidently. "I do. And this time, we'll make sure our recipes are locked up tighter than Fort Knox."

They laughed, the sound of their joy mixing with the gentle clinking of dishes being put away. As they turned off the lights and locked the door, Morty felt a deep sense of gratitude wash over him. For his family, his loyal customers, and yes, even for the hard lessons they'd learned along the way.

The stolen recipe fiasco had been a blessing in disguise. It had taught them the importance of vigilance, the value of trust, and the strength they possessed as a team. As they walked hand in hand towards their car, Morty knew that whatever challenges lay ahead, they would face them together, just as they always had.

And so, The Ghoulish Gourmet continued to grow and flourish, a testament to Morty and Willow's resilience, creativity, and unwavering passion for their craft. The future, with all its possibilities, beckoned brightly before them.

ABOUT PATTI

Ladies and gentlemen, step right up to "Where the Magic Happens" - a literary circus that'll make your bookshelf do backflips!

Meet Patti, the ringmaster of this wordy wonderland! She's not just an Executive Producer; she's a word-wrangling wizard, conjuring up an animated TV series based on "ELLIOT FINDS A HOME." It's the tail-wagging tale of a thumbs-up pup and his silent sidekick, proving that you don't need words when you've got opposable digits and a heart of gold!

Hold onto your bestseller lists, folks! This Polygon Entertainment superstar has hit the USA TODAY jackpot and Amazon's #1 spot more times than a cat has lives. With 7 dozen books under her belt, she's got more genres than a chameleon has colors. From Urban Fantasy to Horror, she's been spinning yarns longer than your grandma's knitting needles!

But wait, there's more! Patti's life is like a celebrity bingo card:

She rocked "Romper Room" at 4, probably making the other kids look like amateur rompers.

She rubbed elbows with Captain Kangaroo and Mr. Green Jeans. (No word on whether the jeans were actually green.)

She shared a train ride and a sandwich with Sidney Poitier. Talk about a meal ticket to stardom!

She high-fived President Nixon at the circus. Who knew the circus could get any more political?

She went to school with David Copperfield. We assume she didn't disappear during attendance.

She roller-skated with pre-famous John Travolta. Grease lightning, indeed!

She sipped cocoa with Abe Vigoda. Fish never tasted so sweet!

When she's not busy being a literary legend, Patti's juggling roles faster than a circus performer. Teacher, grandma, furparent - she does it all with a smile that could light up a haunted house.

Speaking of haunted houses, meet the "Queen of Halloween" herself! This Wiccan High Priestess is stirring up stories spookier than a skeleton's dance moves. Her books are flying off the shelves faster than witches on broomsticks, so follow her on social media or risk missing out on the hocus-pocus!

So, come one, come all, to Patti's phantasmagorical world of words! It's more exciting than a roller coaster, more magical than a rabbit in a hat, and more diverse than a box of assorted chocolates. Don't be shy - step into the spotlight and join the literary party where the pages turn themselves and the stories never end!

www.ingramcontent.com/pod-product-compliance
Lightning Source LLC
LaVergne TN
LVHW092051060526
838201LV00047B/1331